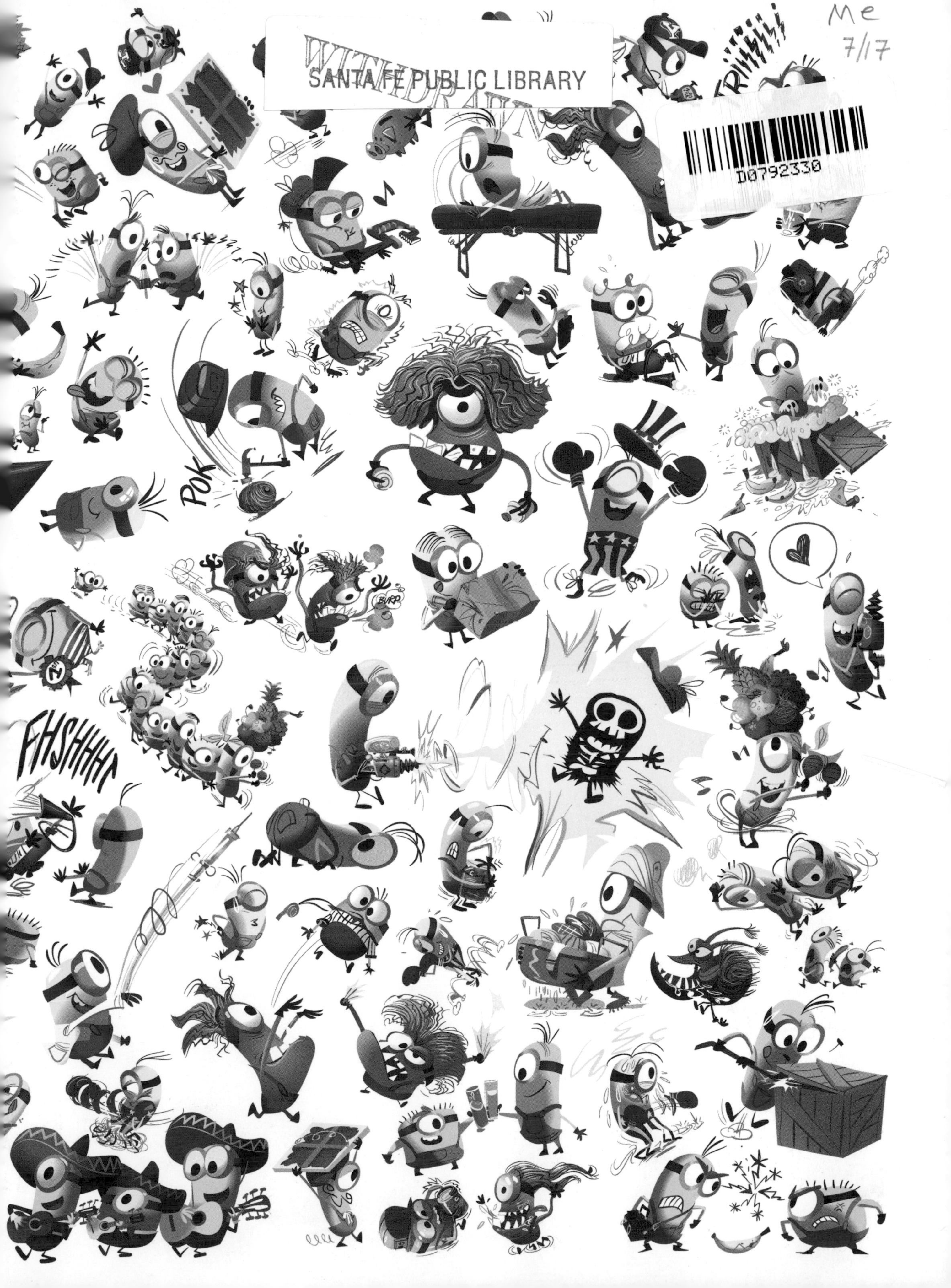
POK
BURP

MINIONS

EVIL PANIC!

Art by: Renaud COLLIN   **Written by: Stéphane LAPUSS'**

Based on the characters from Universal Pictures and Illumination Entertainment's 2010 animated theatrical motion picture, "Despicable Me", the 2013 animated theatrical motion picture entitled "Despicable Me 2", and the 2015 animated theatrical motion picture release presently entitled "Minions".

TITAN COMICS

Senior Editor
NATALIE CLUBB

Designer
RUSSELL SEAL

Studio Manager
SELINA JUNEJA

Production Supervisors
PETER JAMES, JACKIE FLOOK
MARIA PEARSON

Production Manager
OBI ONUORA

Senior Sales Manager
STEVE TOTHILL

Commercial Manager
MICHELLE FAIRLAMB

Direct Sales & Marketing Manager
RICKY CLAYDON

Publishing Manager
DARRYL TOTHILL

Publishing Director
CHRIS TEATHER

Operations Director
LEIGH BAULCH

Executive Director
VIVIAN CHEUNG

Publisher
NICK LANDAU

ISBN: 9781782765561

Published by Titan Comics,
a division of Titan Publishing Group Ltd.
144 Southwark St. London, SE1 0UP

10 9 8 7 6 5 4 3 2 1
Printed in China, January 2016
A CIP catalogue record for this title is available from the British Library.
Titan Comics. TCN0865

**Also available from Titan Comics
Minions Volume 1 - Banana!
www.titan-comics.com**

EVIL MINION

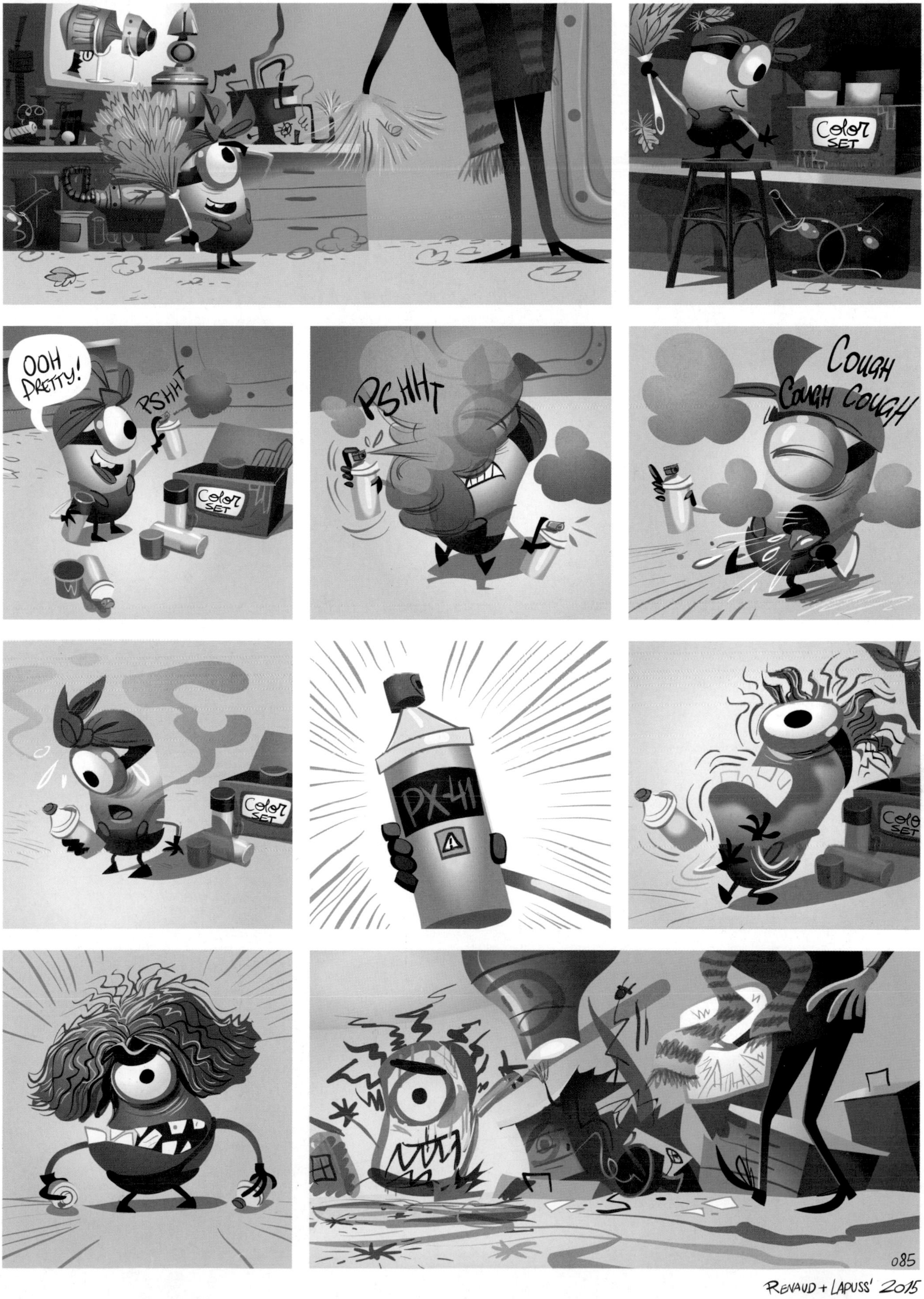
Color SET
OOH PRETTY!
PSHHT
PSHHT
COUGH
COUGH COUGH
PX-41

RENAUD + LAPUSS' 2015

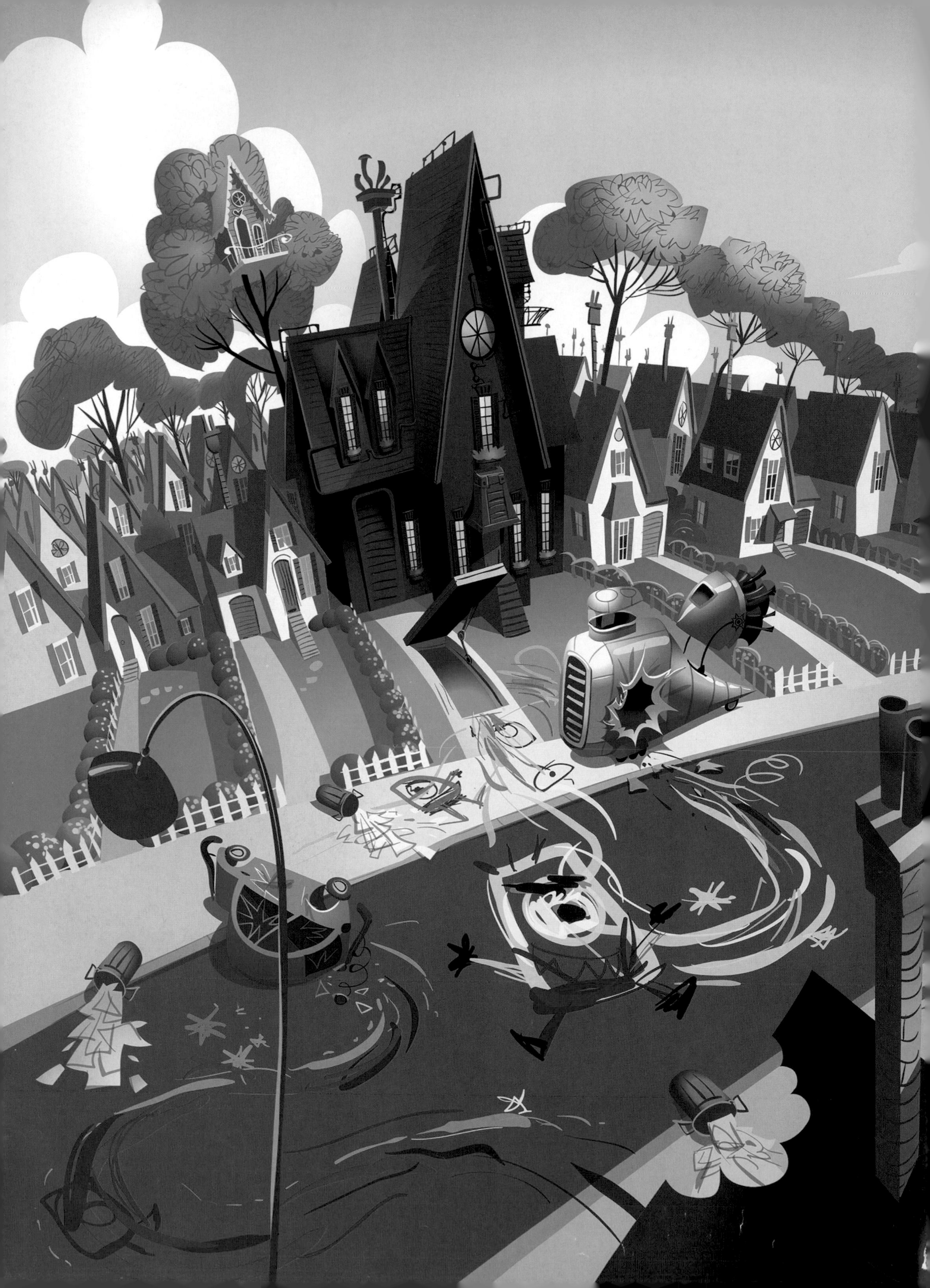

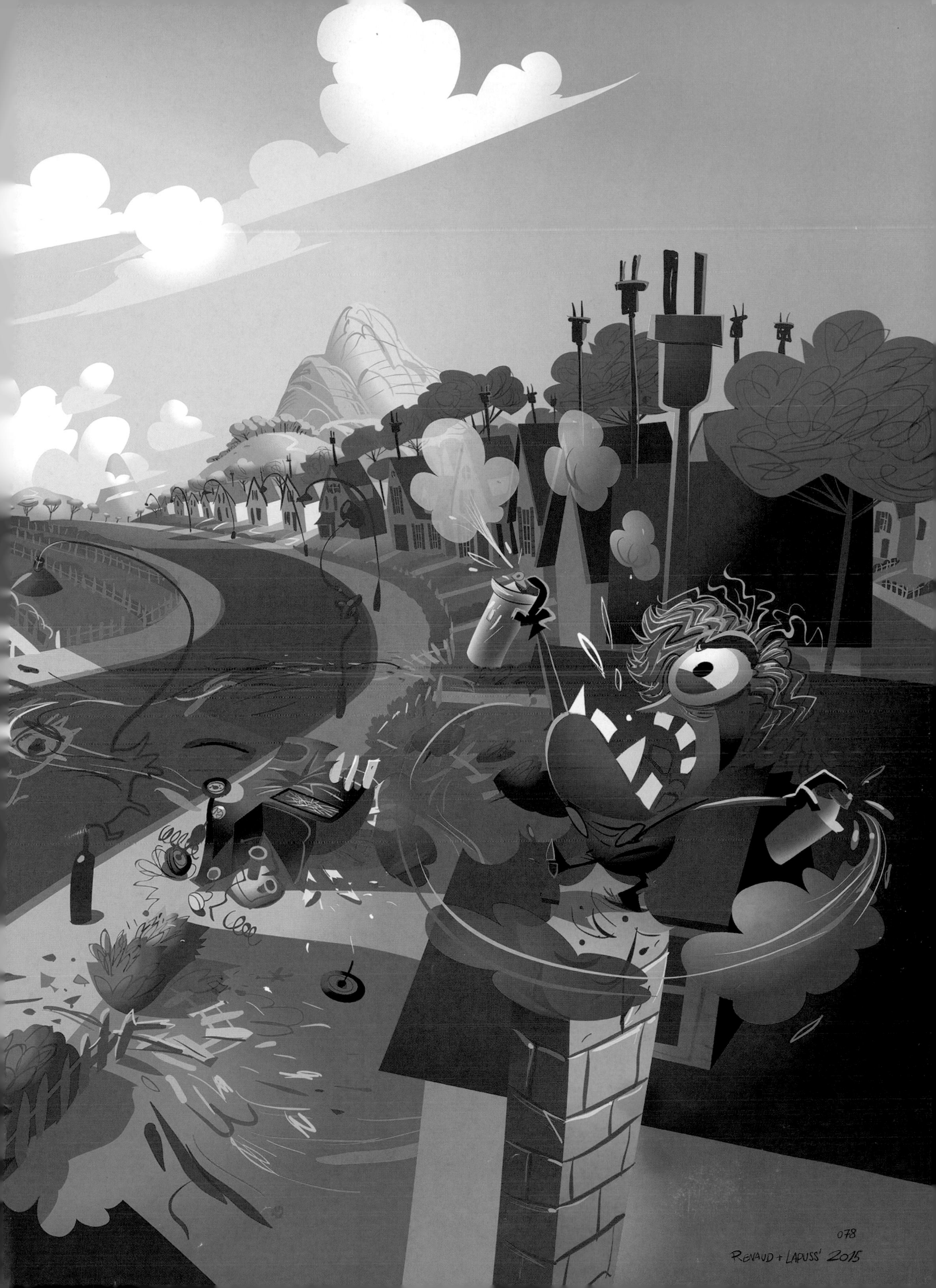
REVAUD + LAPUSS' 2015

AN EYE FOR AN EYE

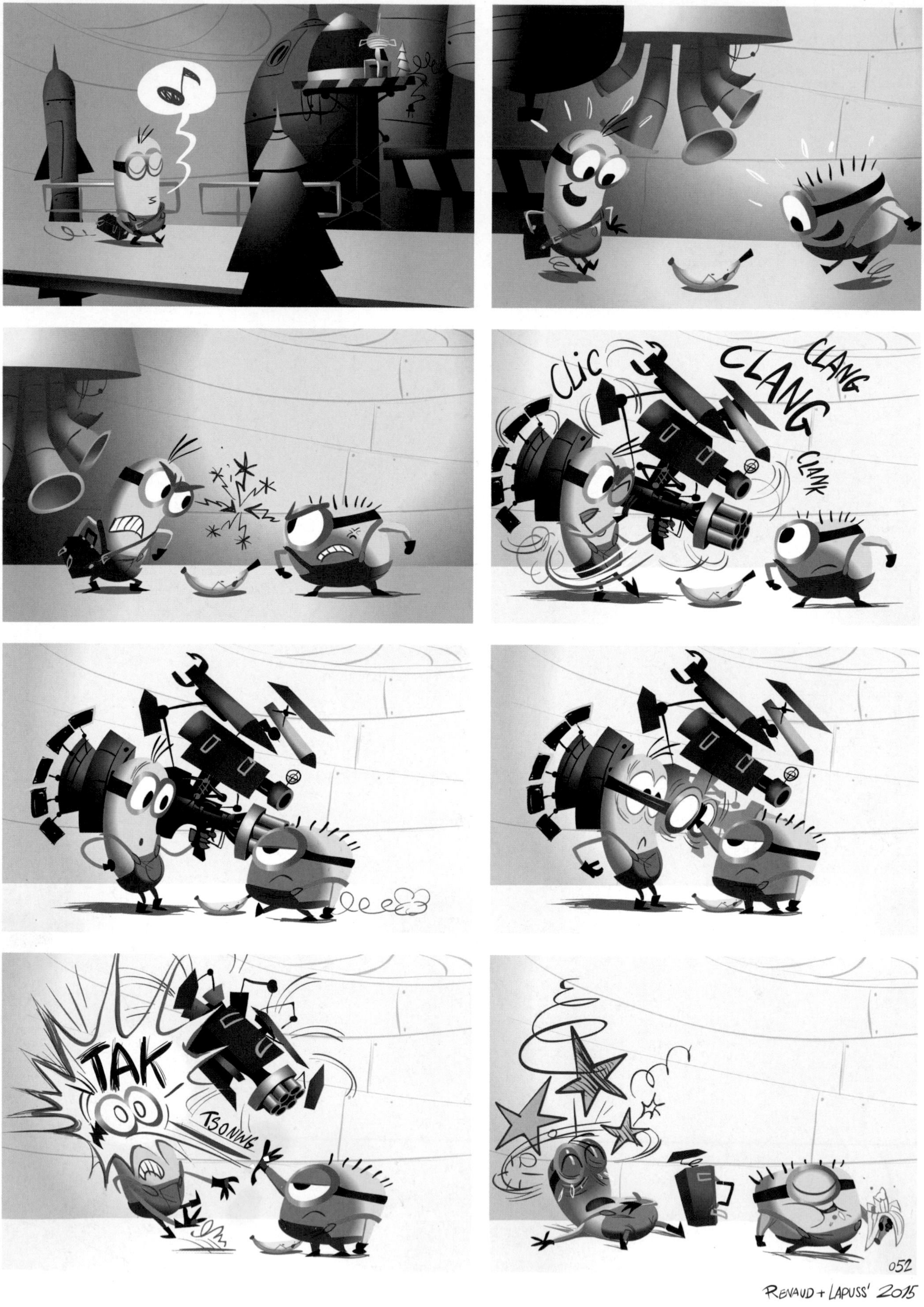
CLIC
CLANG
CLANG
CLANK
TAK
TSONNG

REVAUD + LAPUSS' 2015

BZZZZZ

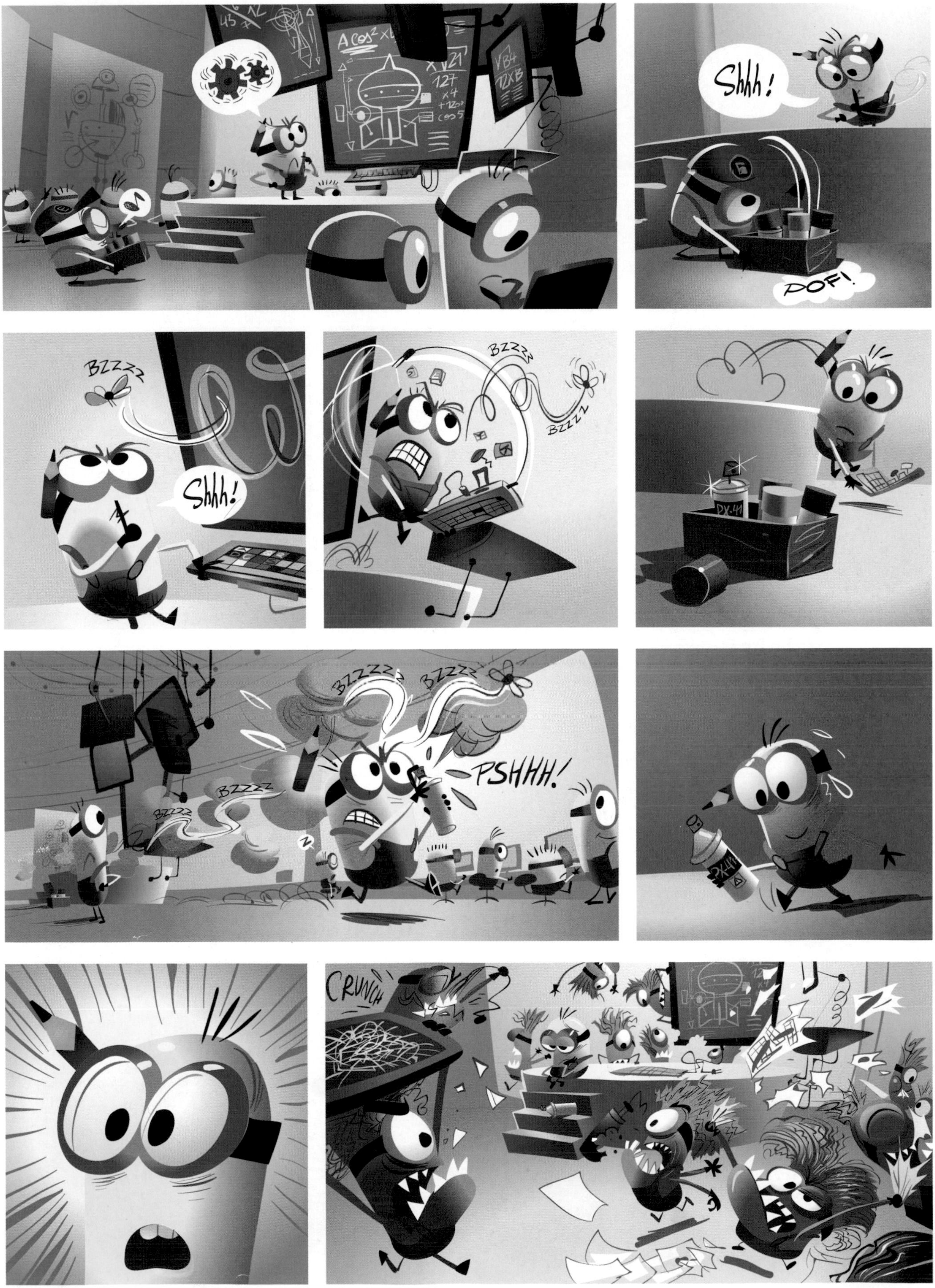

Shhh!
POF!
BZZZZ
Shhh!
BZZZZ
BZZZZ
BZZZZZ
BZZZZ
PSHHH!
BZZZZ
BZZZZ
CRUNCH

RENAUD + LAPUSS' 2015

CHEERS!

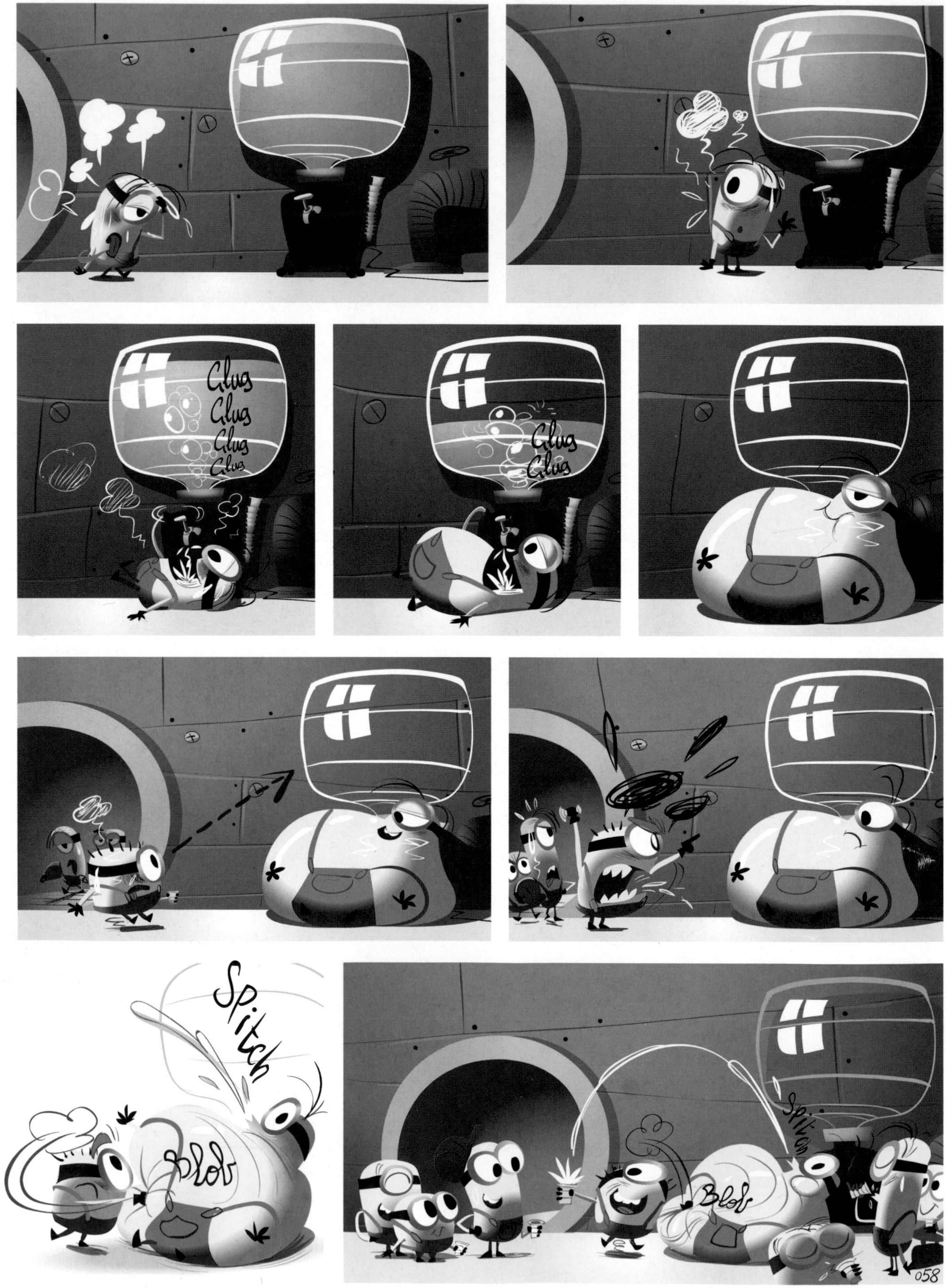
Glug
Glug
Glug
Glug
Glug
Glug
Spitch
Blob
Spitch
Blob
058

RENAUD + LAPUSS' 2015

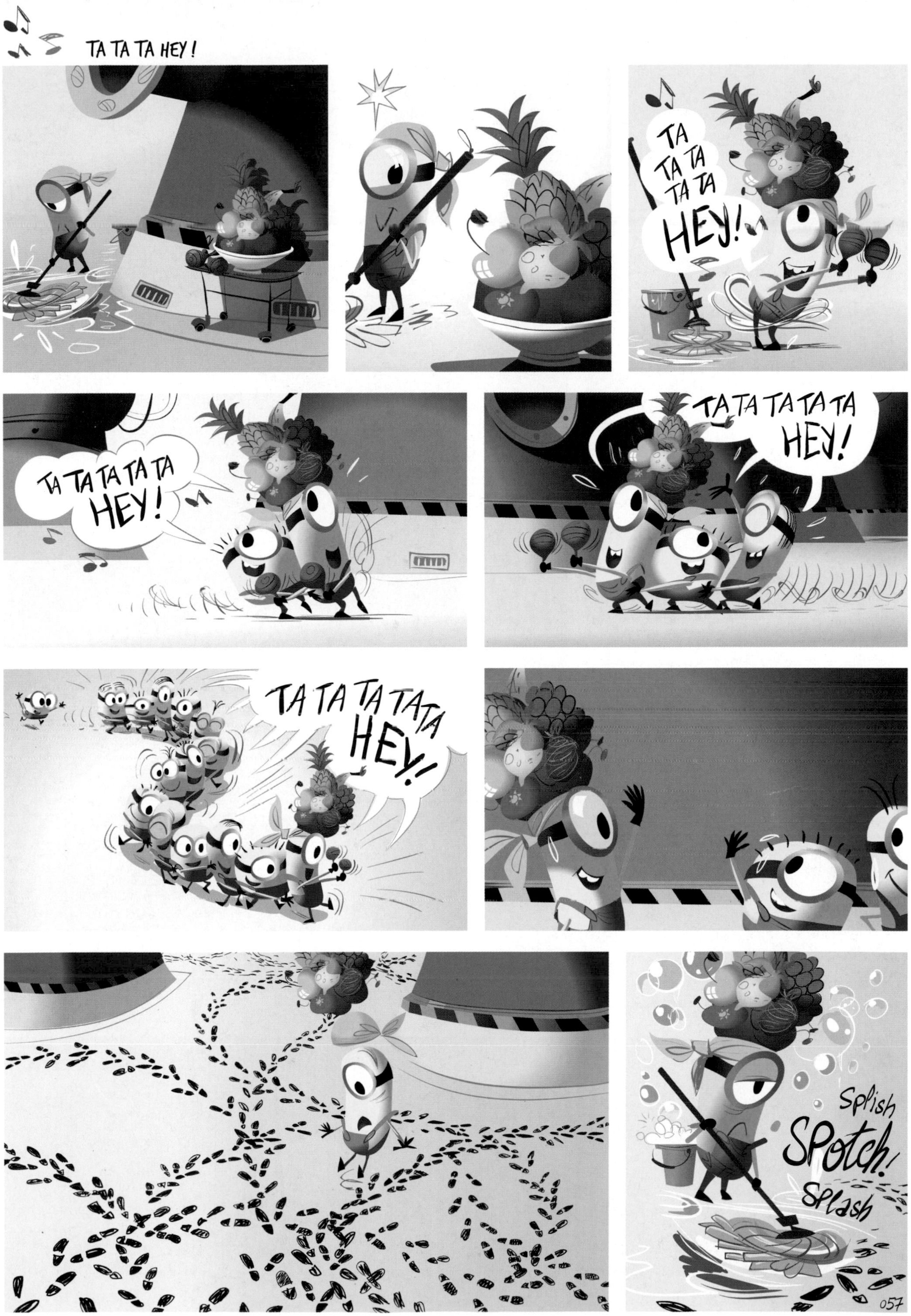
TA TA TA HEY !
TA TA TA TA TA HEY!
TA TA TA TA TA HEY!
TA TA TA TA TA HEY!
TA TA TA TA TA HEY!
Splish
SPotch!
Splash

RENAUD + LAPUSS' 2015

ON THE ROCKS

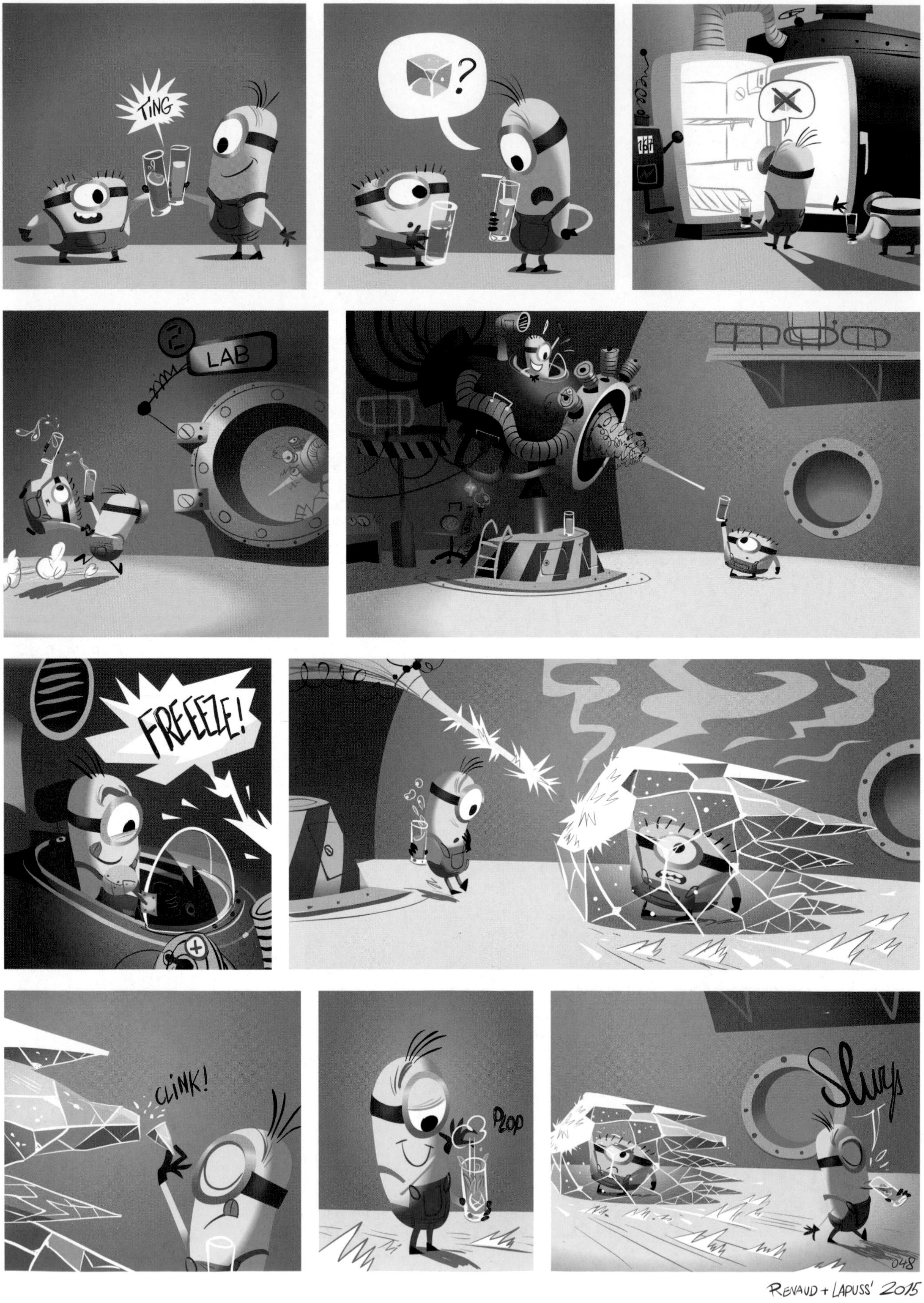

TING
?
2
LAB
FREEEZE!
CLINK!
PLOP
Slurp
048

RENAUD + LAPUSS' 2015

BBQ PARTY

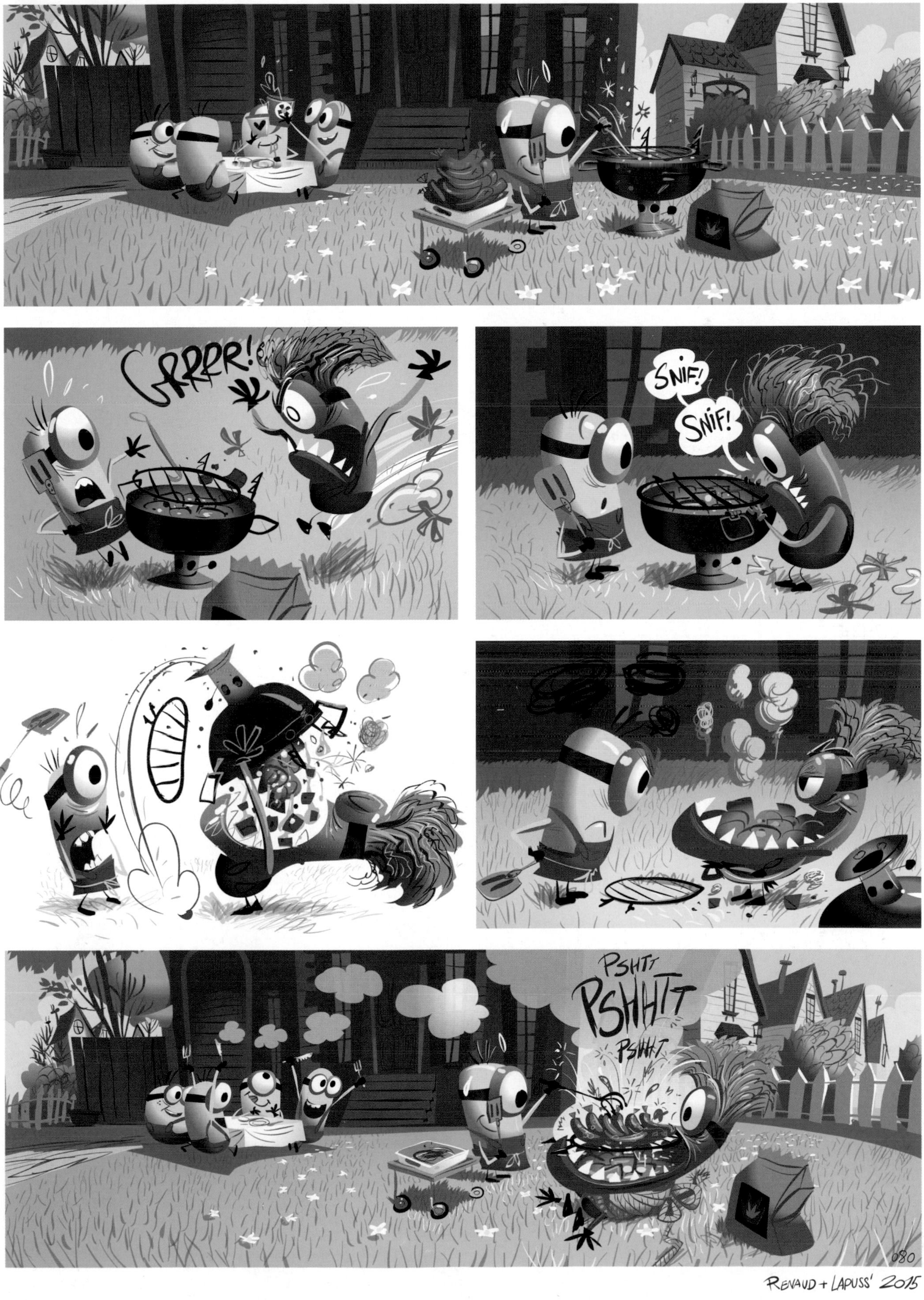
GRRRR!
SNIF!
SNIF!
PSHTT
PSHHTT
PSHHT

RENAUD + LAPUSS' 2015

FRAGILE

HOPELA !

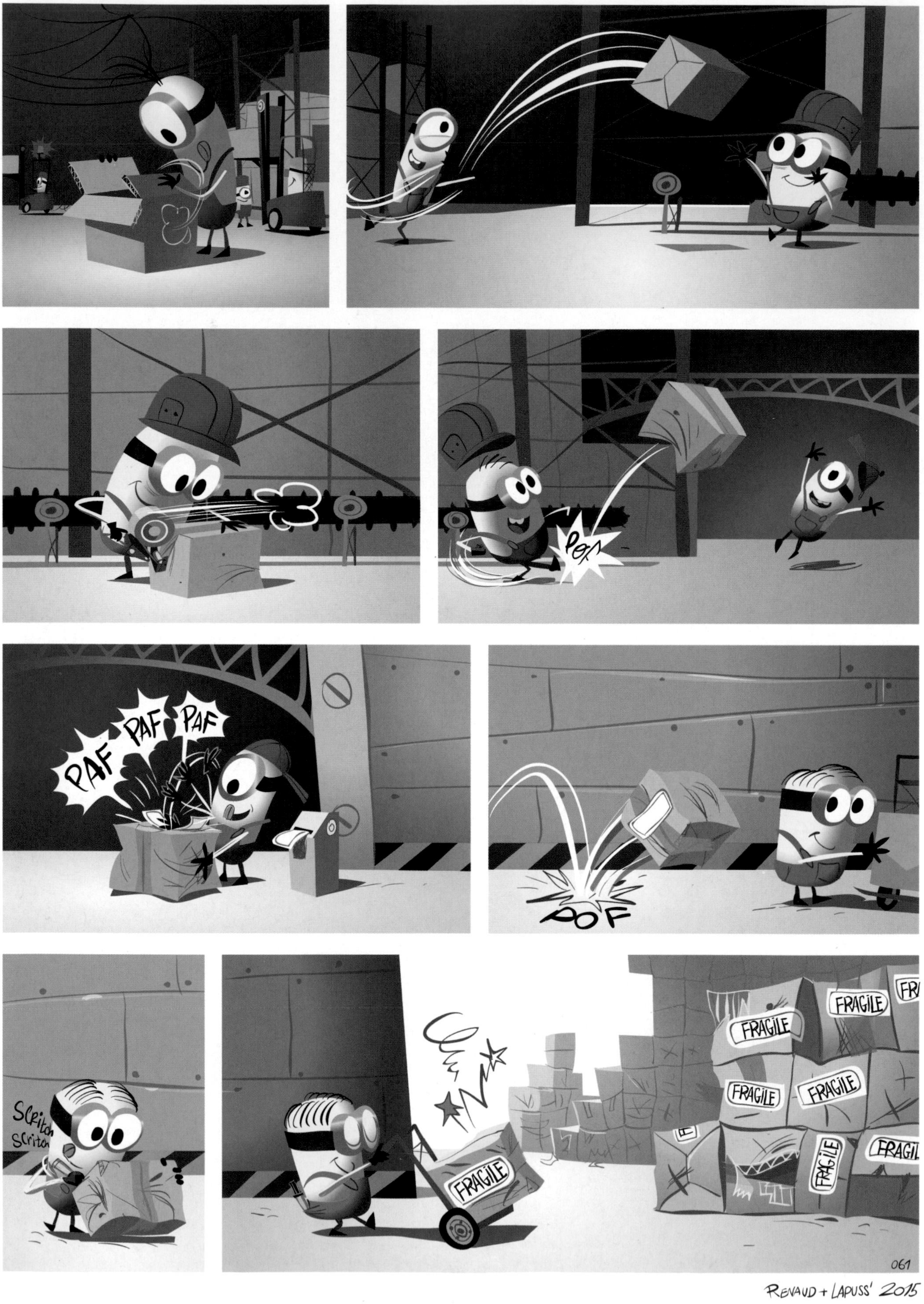
Pof
PAF
PAF
PAF
POF
SCRITCH
SCRITCH
FRAGILE
FRAGILE
FRAGILE
FRAGILE
FRAGILE
FRAGILE
FRAGILE

RENAUD + LAPUSS' 2015

FULL BACK

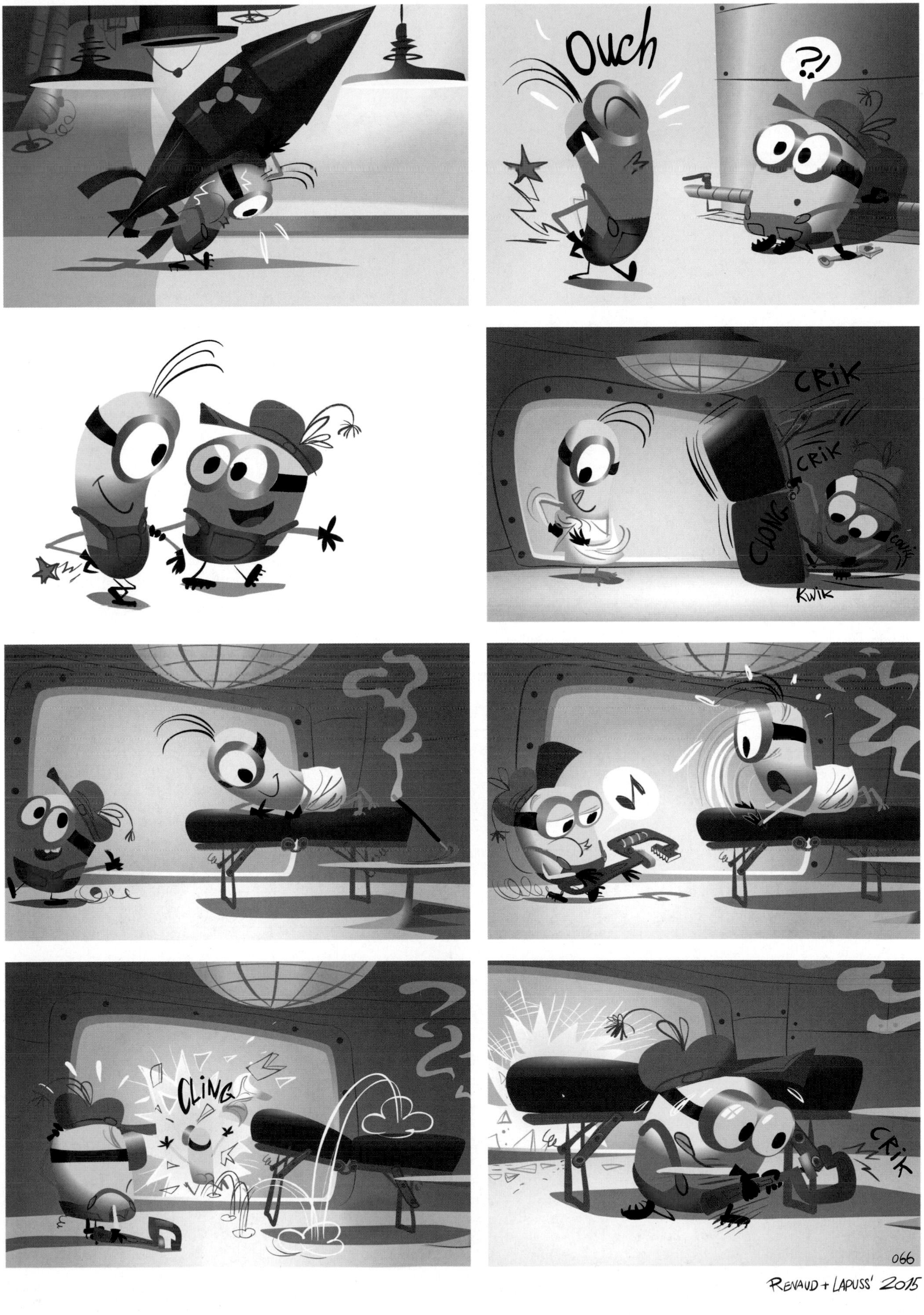
Ouch
?!
CRIK
CRIK
CLONG
KWIK
CLING
CRIK

RENAUD + LAPUSS' 2015

NO MILK TODAY

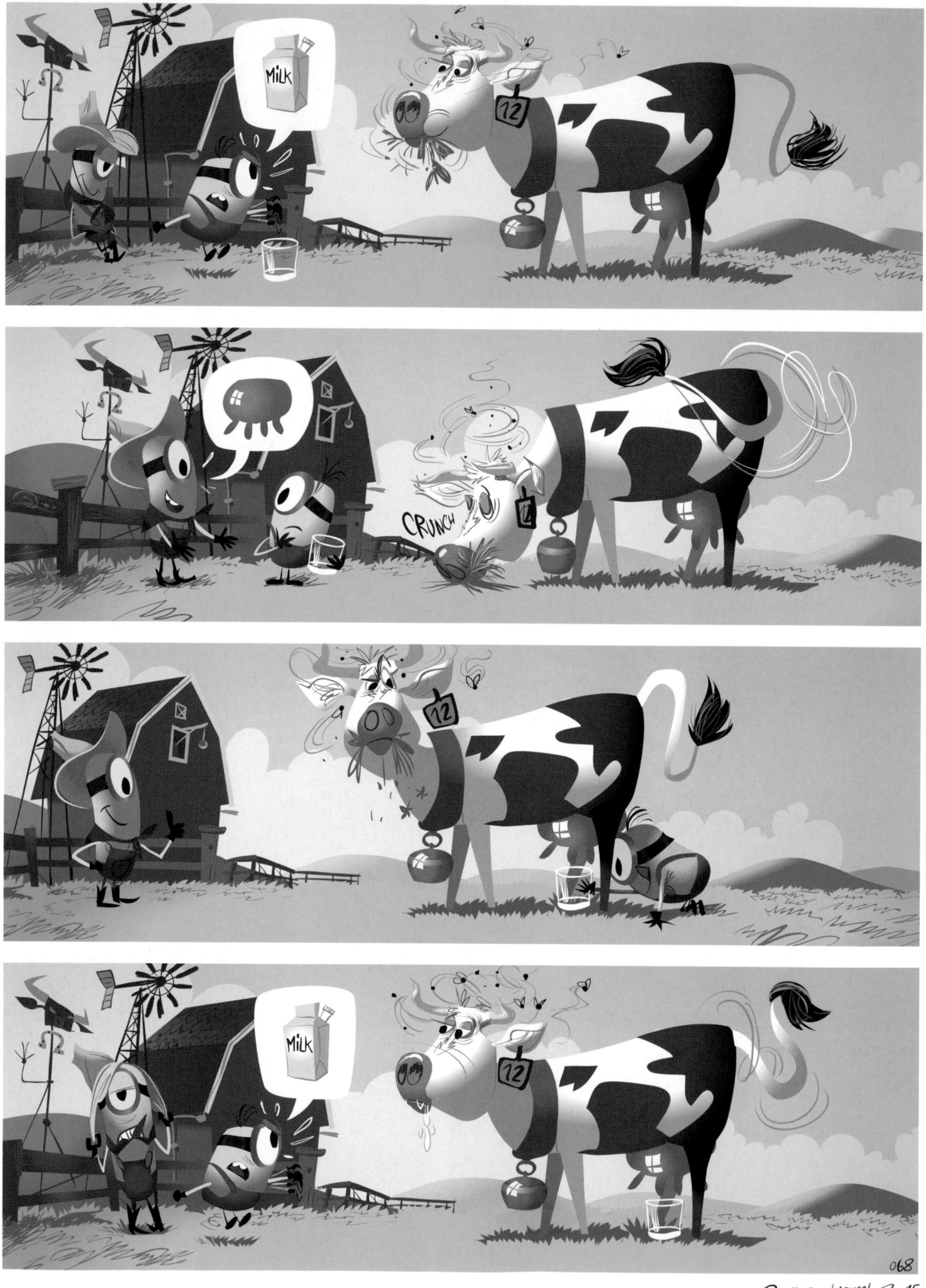
MILK
12
CRUNCH
12
12
MILK
12

RENAUD + LAPUSS' 2015

FIRE ALARM

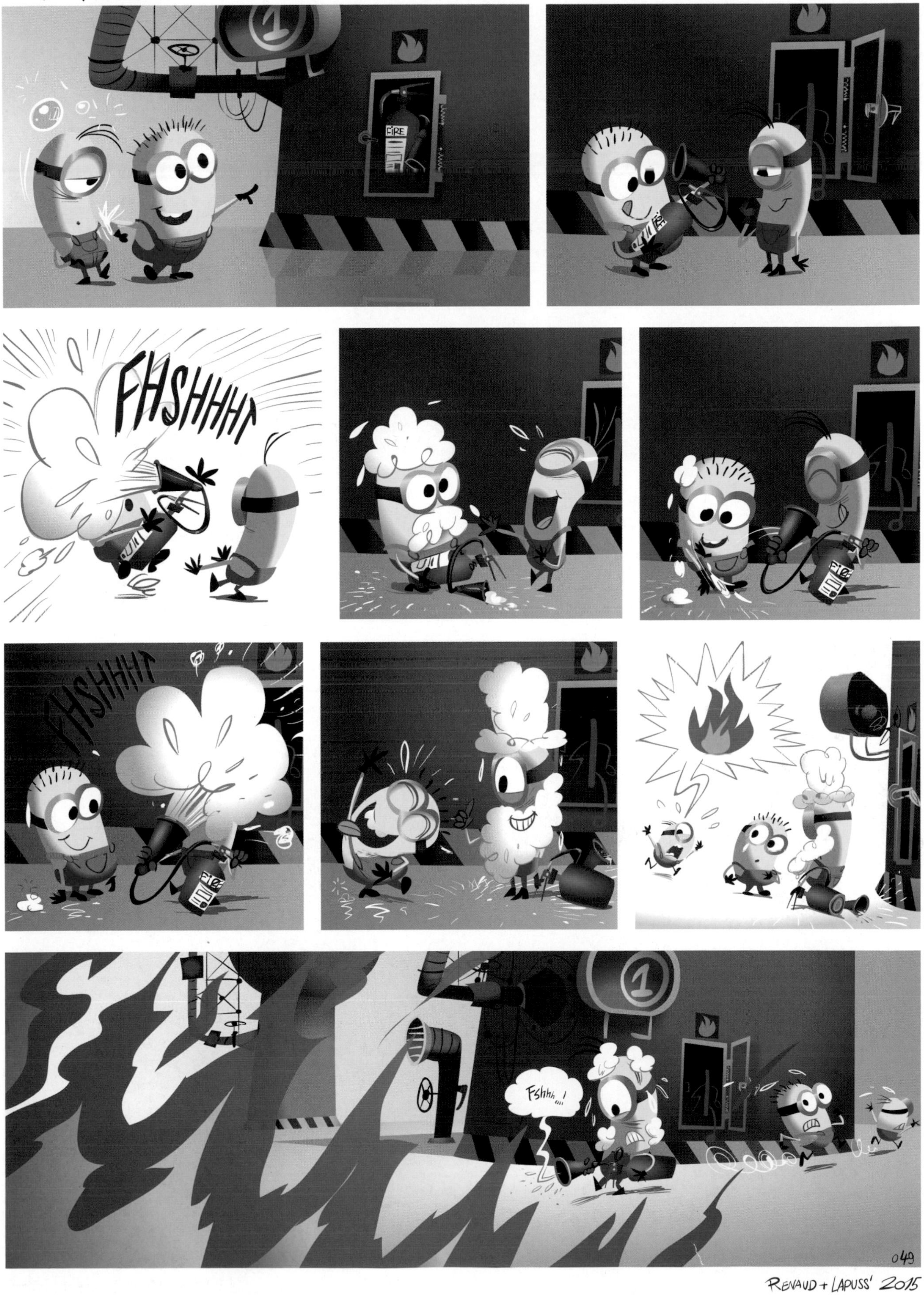

FIRE
FHSHHHT
FHSHHHT
Fshhh..!

Renaud + Lapuss' 2015

BANANAAAH !

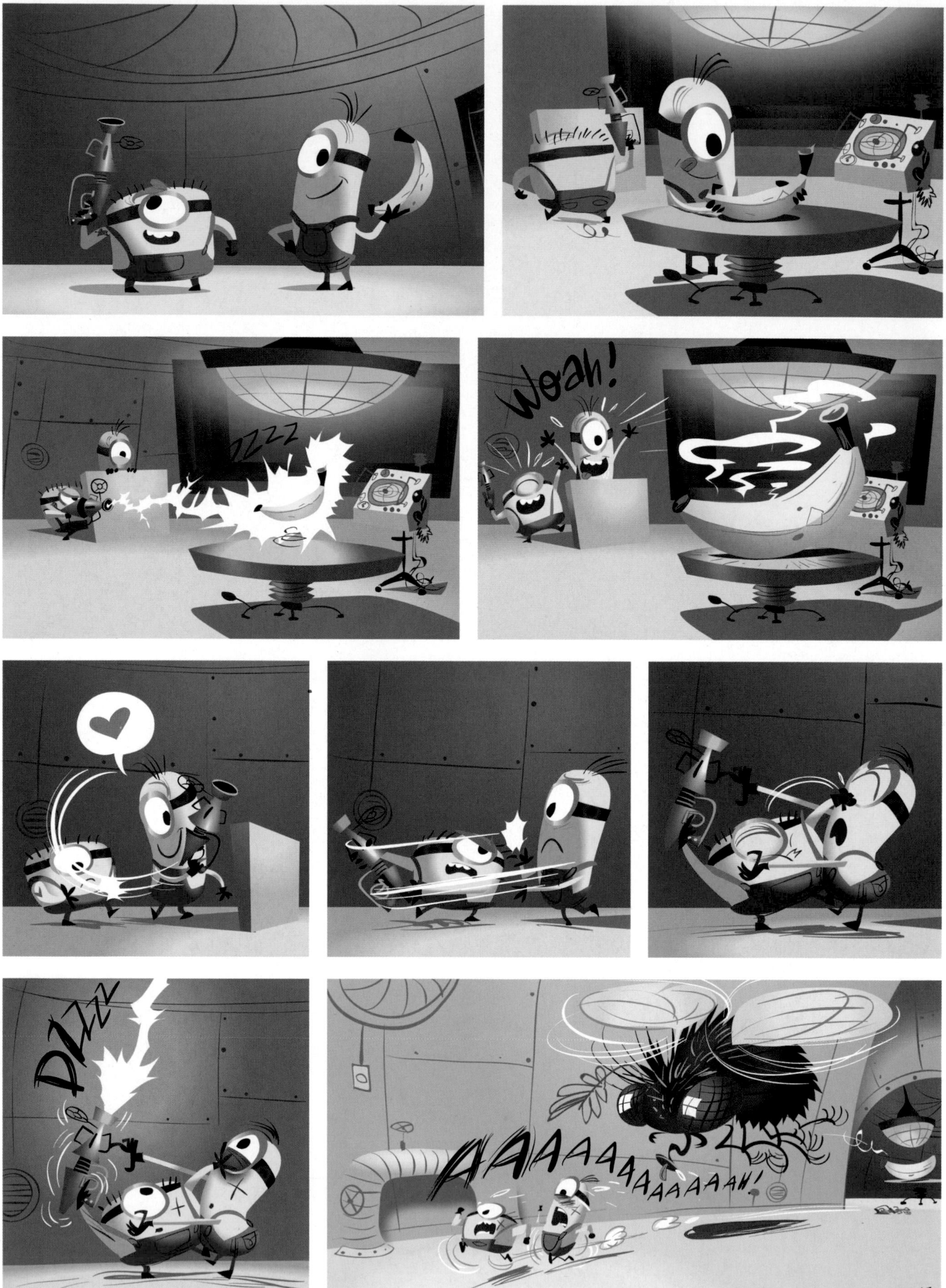
ZZZZ
Woah!
AAAAAAAAAAAAAAH!

RENAUD + LAPUSS' 2015

ICE CREAM 1

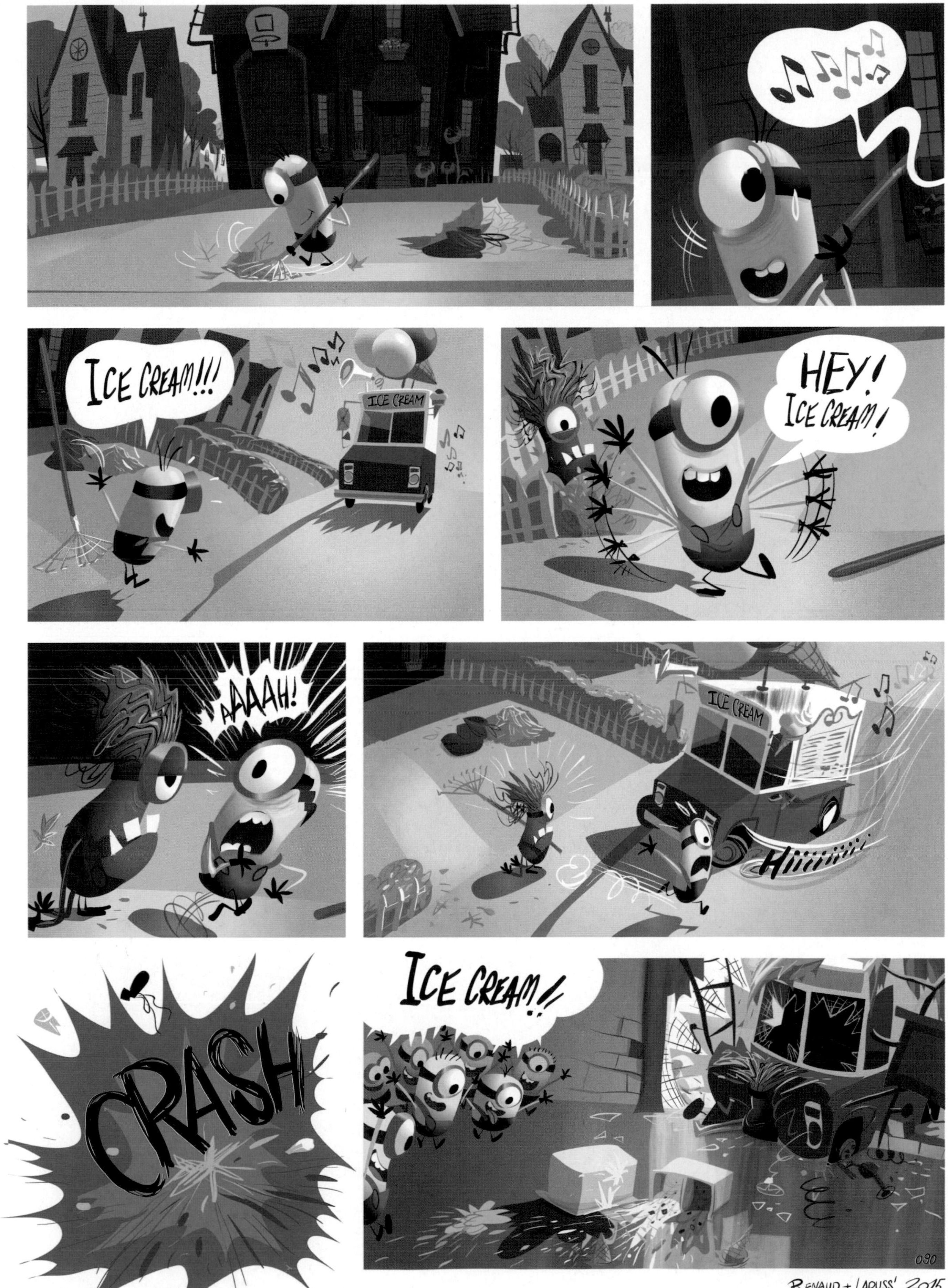
ICE CREAM!!!
ICE CREAM
HEY! ICE CREAM!
AAAAH!
ICE CREAM
Hiiiiiiiiii
CRASH
ICE CREAM!!
090

RENAUD + LAPUSS' 2015

CHERRY ON THE CAKE

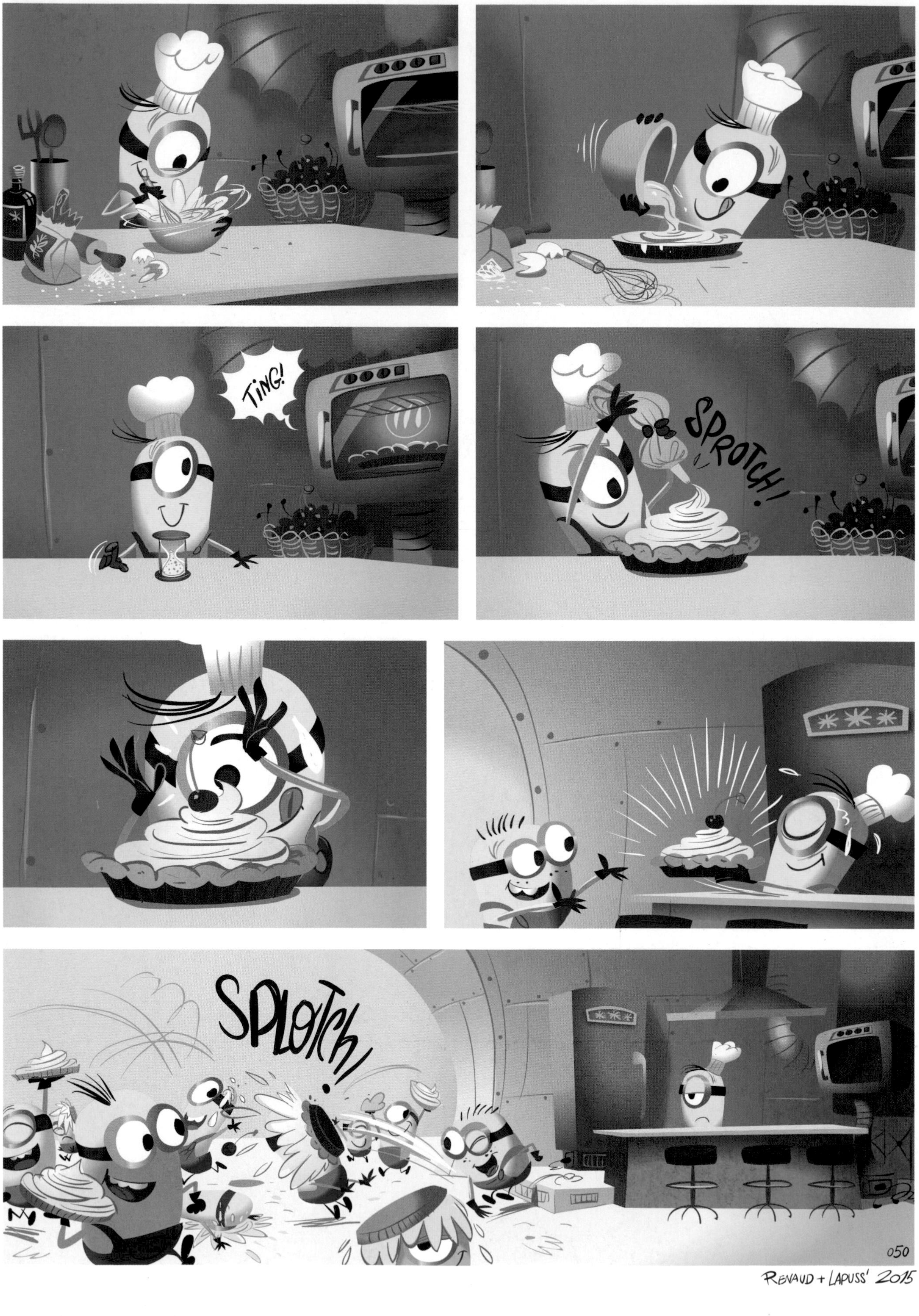

TING!
SPROTCH!
SPLOTCH!

RENAUD + LAPUSS' 2015

THE HEAT IS ON!

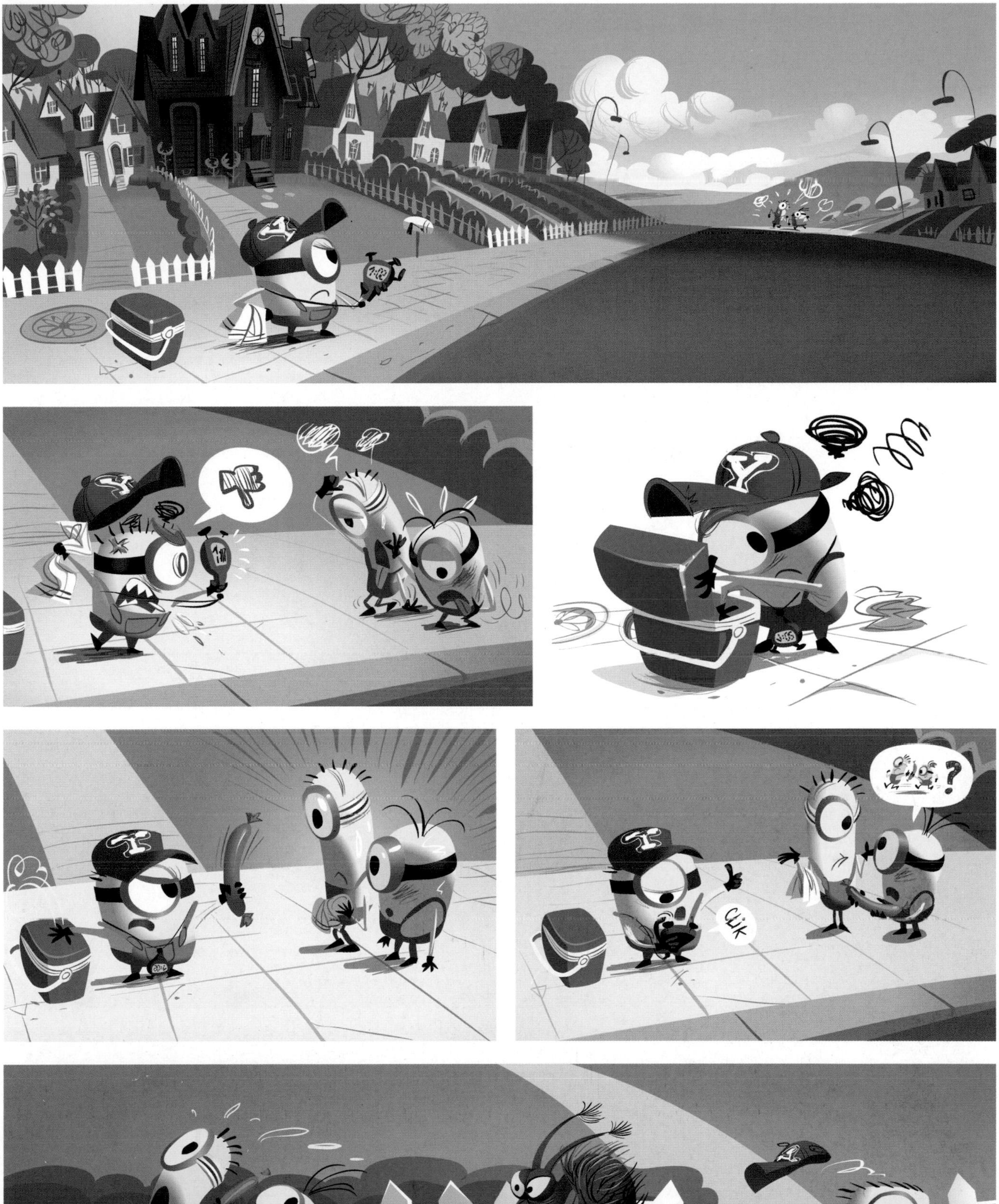

CLIK

RENAUD + LAPUSS' 2015

PIGGY BANK

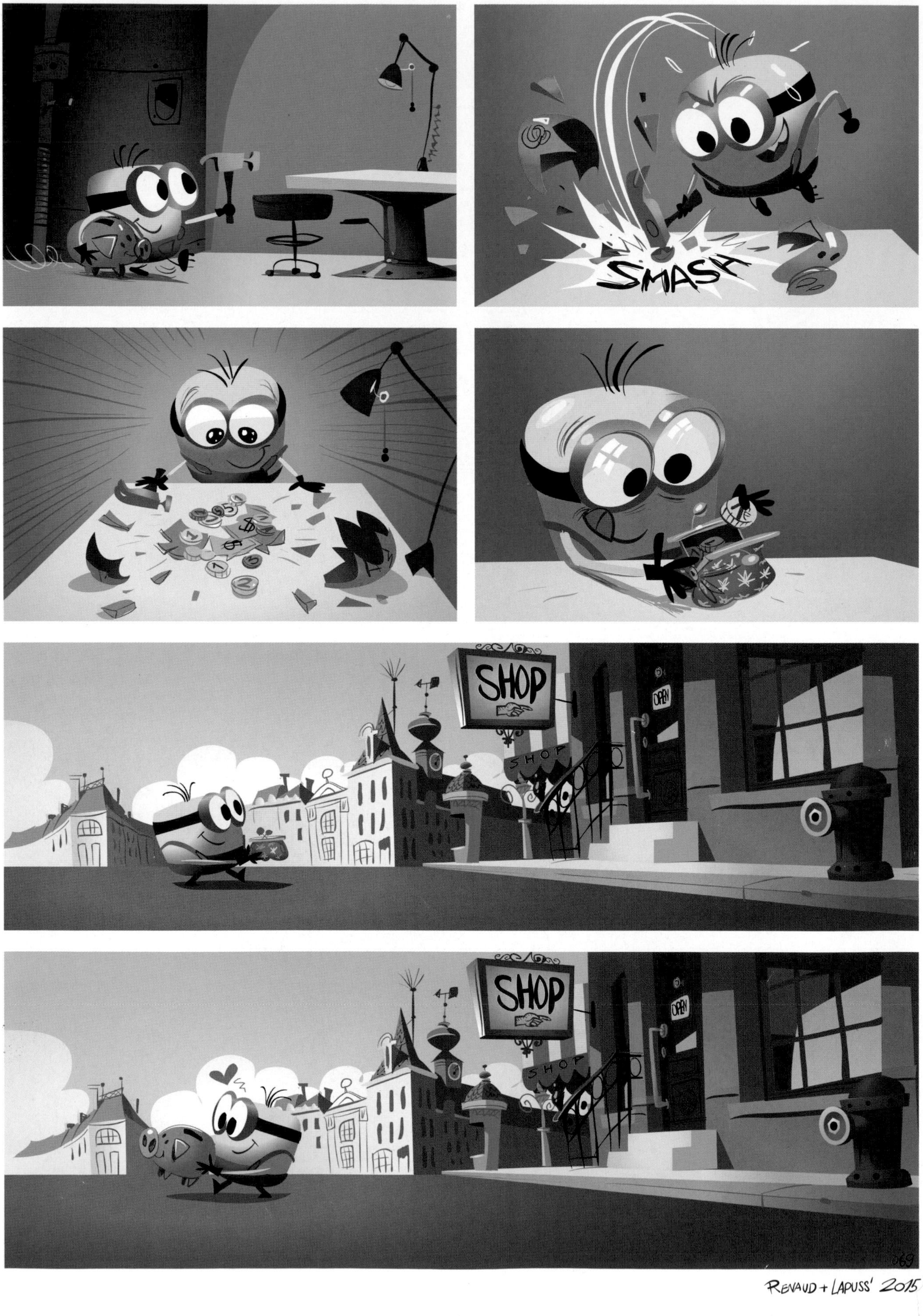
SMASH
SHOP
OPEN
SHOP
SHOP
OPEN
SHOP
069

RENAUD + LAPUSS' 2015

STILL LIFE

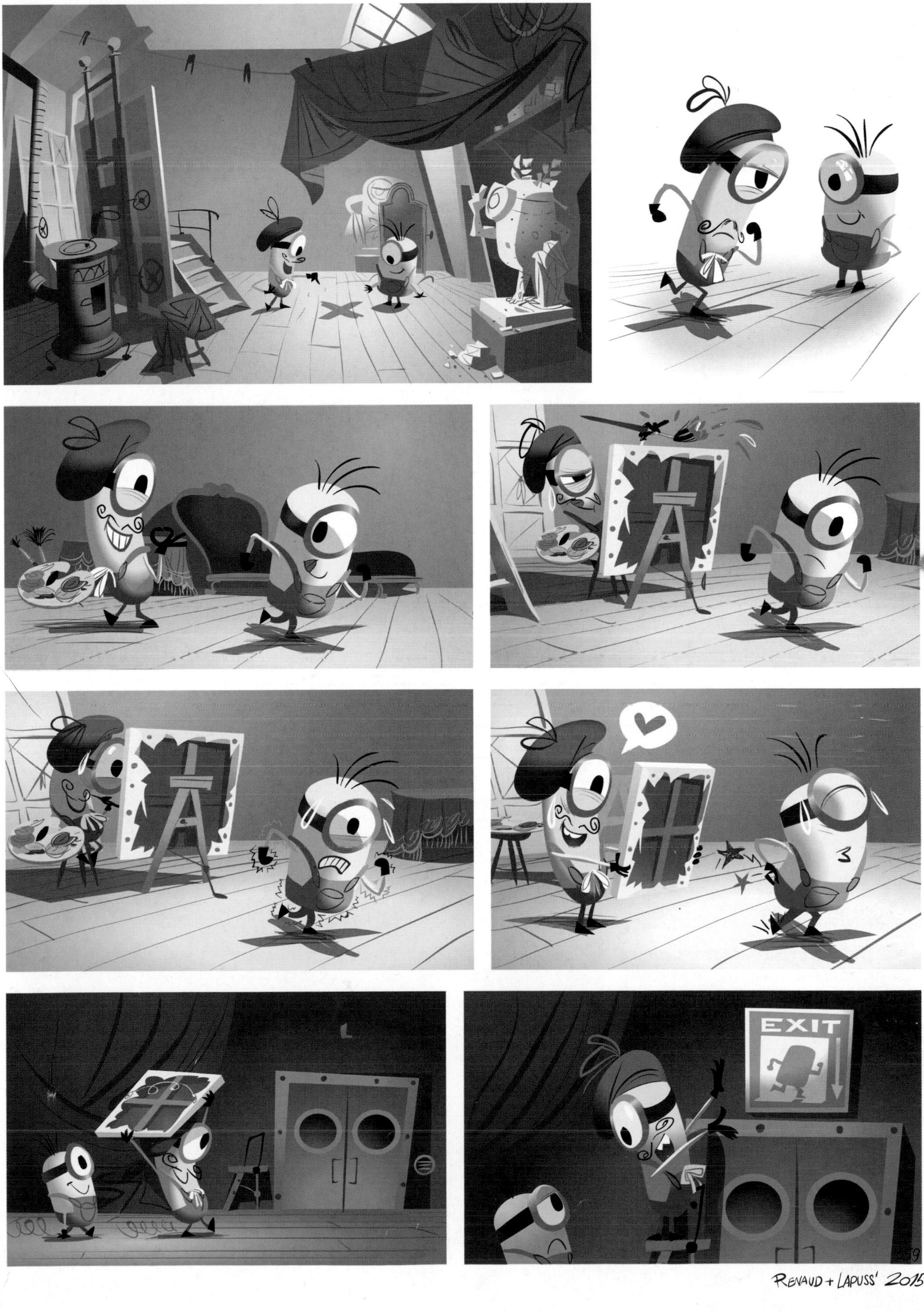
EXIT

RENAUD + LAPUSS' 2015

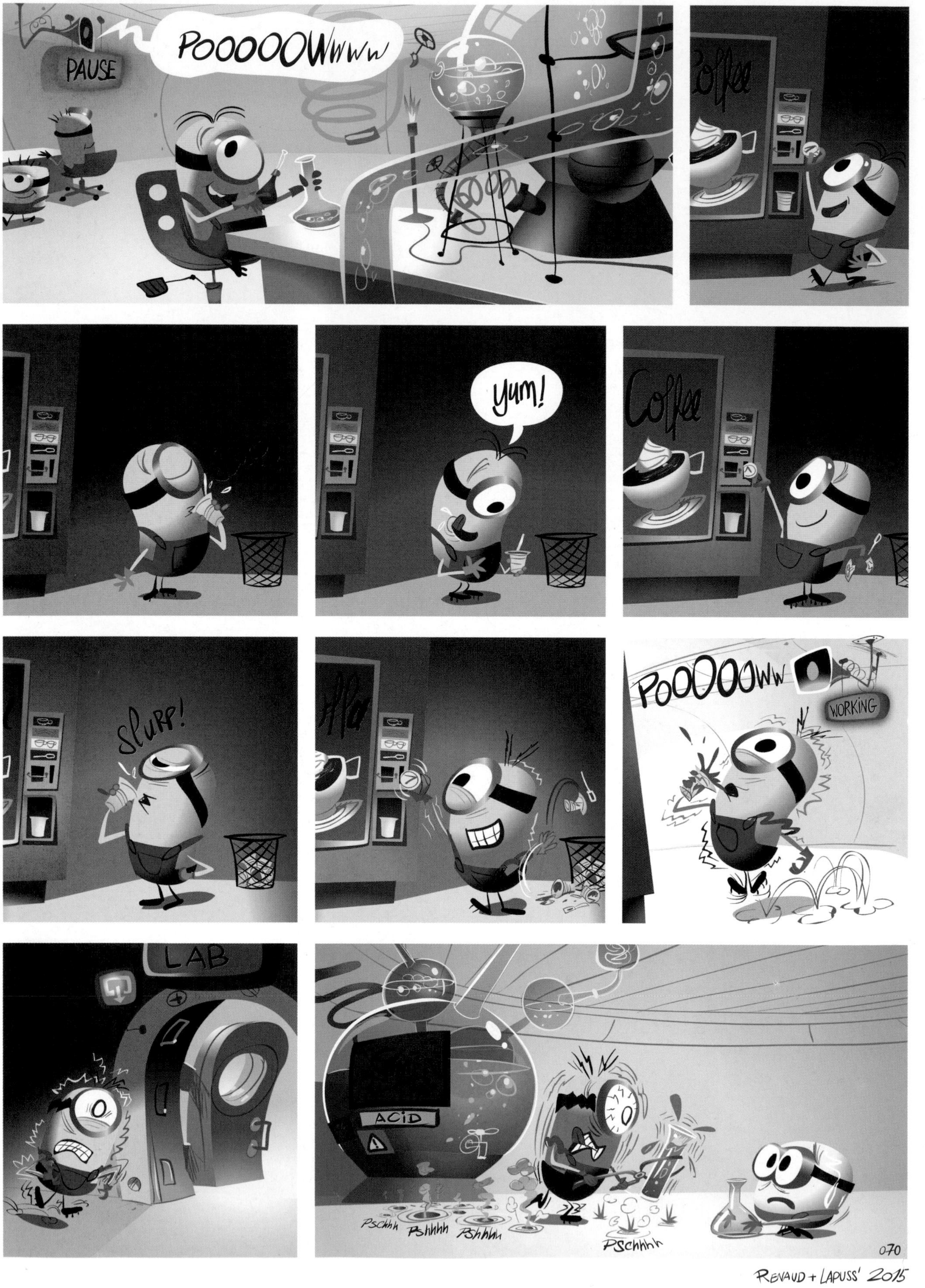
PAUSE
POOOOOWwww
Coffee
Yum!
Coffee
Slurp!
POOOOOww
WORKING
LAB
ACID
Pschhh
Pshhhh
Pshhhh
PSchhhh

RENAUD + LAPUSS' 2015

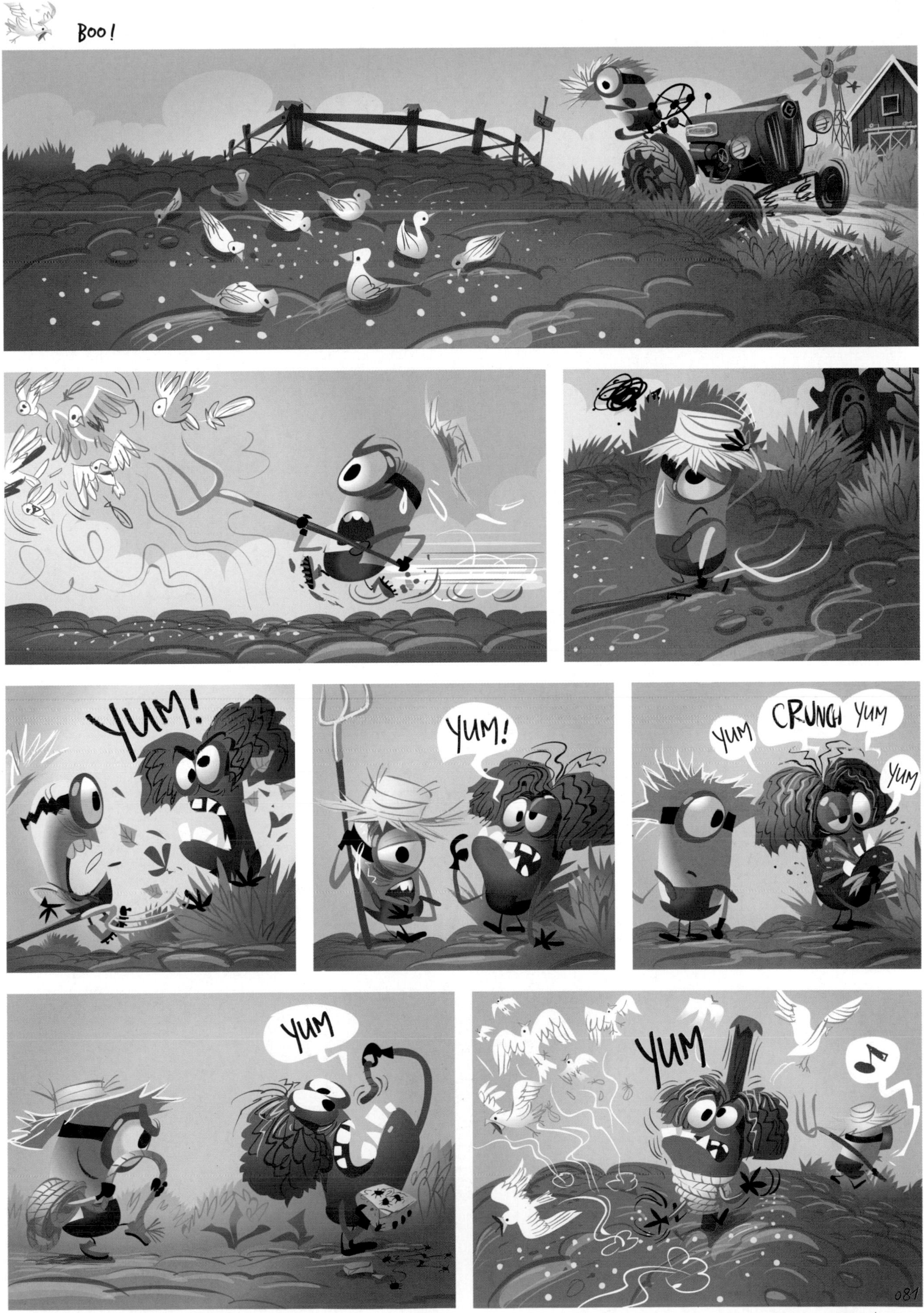
Boo!
YUM!
YUM!
YUM
CRUNCH
YUM
YUM
YUM
YUM

RENAUD + LAPUSS' 2015

KING OF THE RING

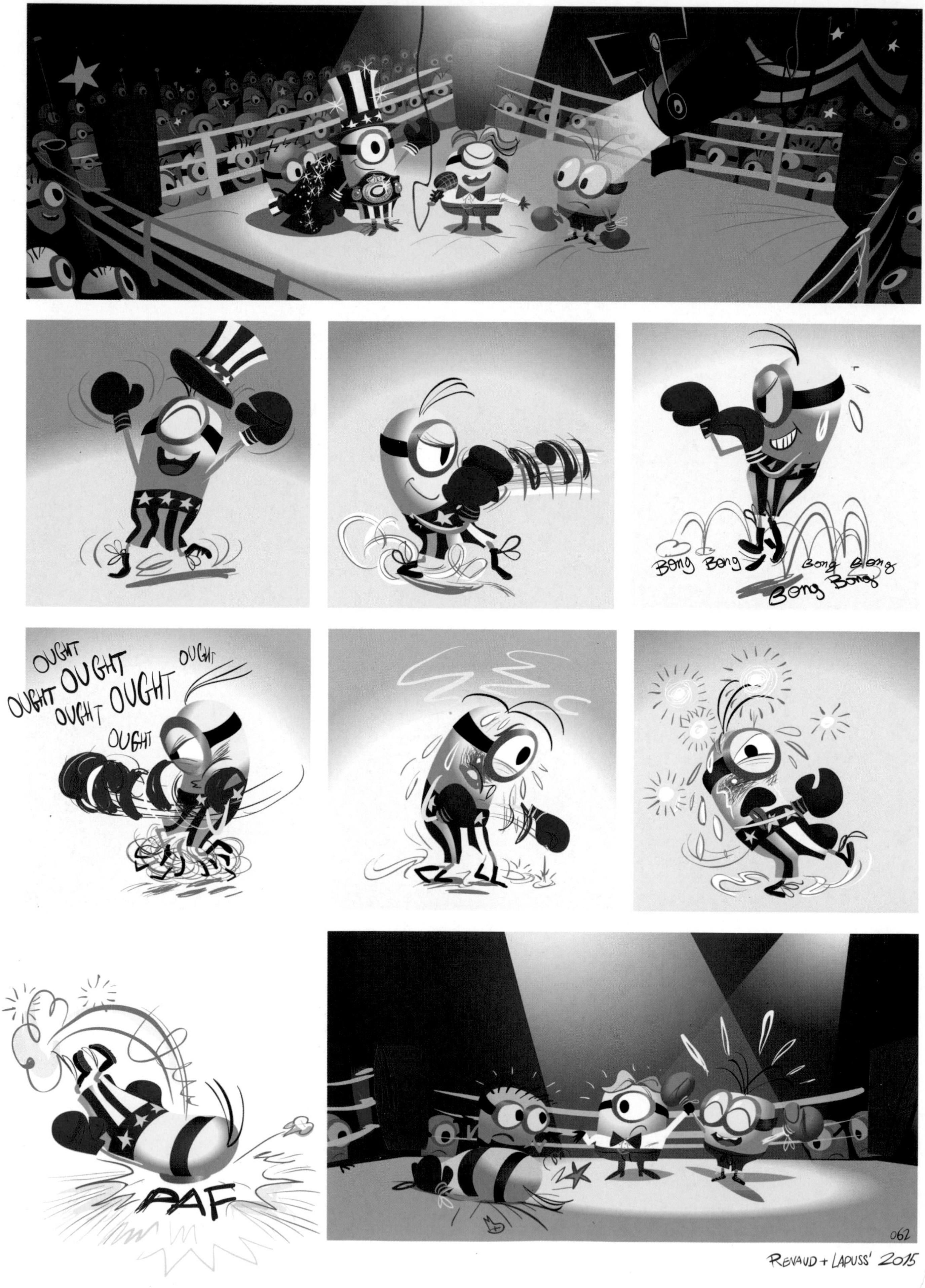
Bong Bong
Bong Bong
Bong Bong
OUGHT
OUGHT OUGHT
OUGHT
OUGHT OUGHT
OUGHT
PAF

RENAUD + LAPUSS' 2015

ICE CREAM II

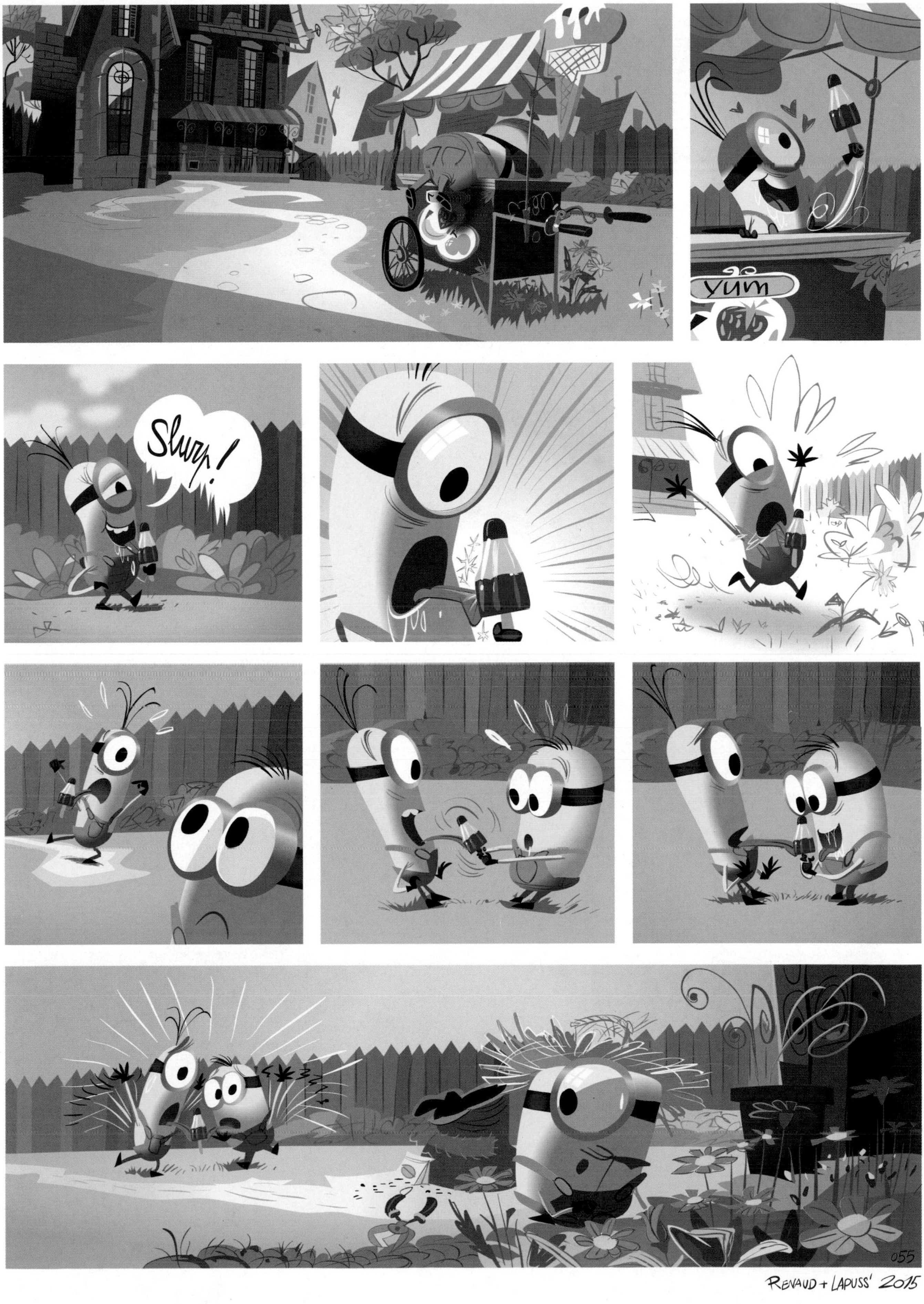
YUM
Slurp!

RENAUD + LAPUSS' 2015

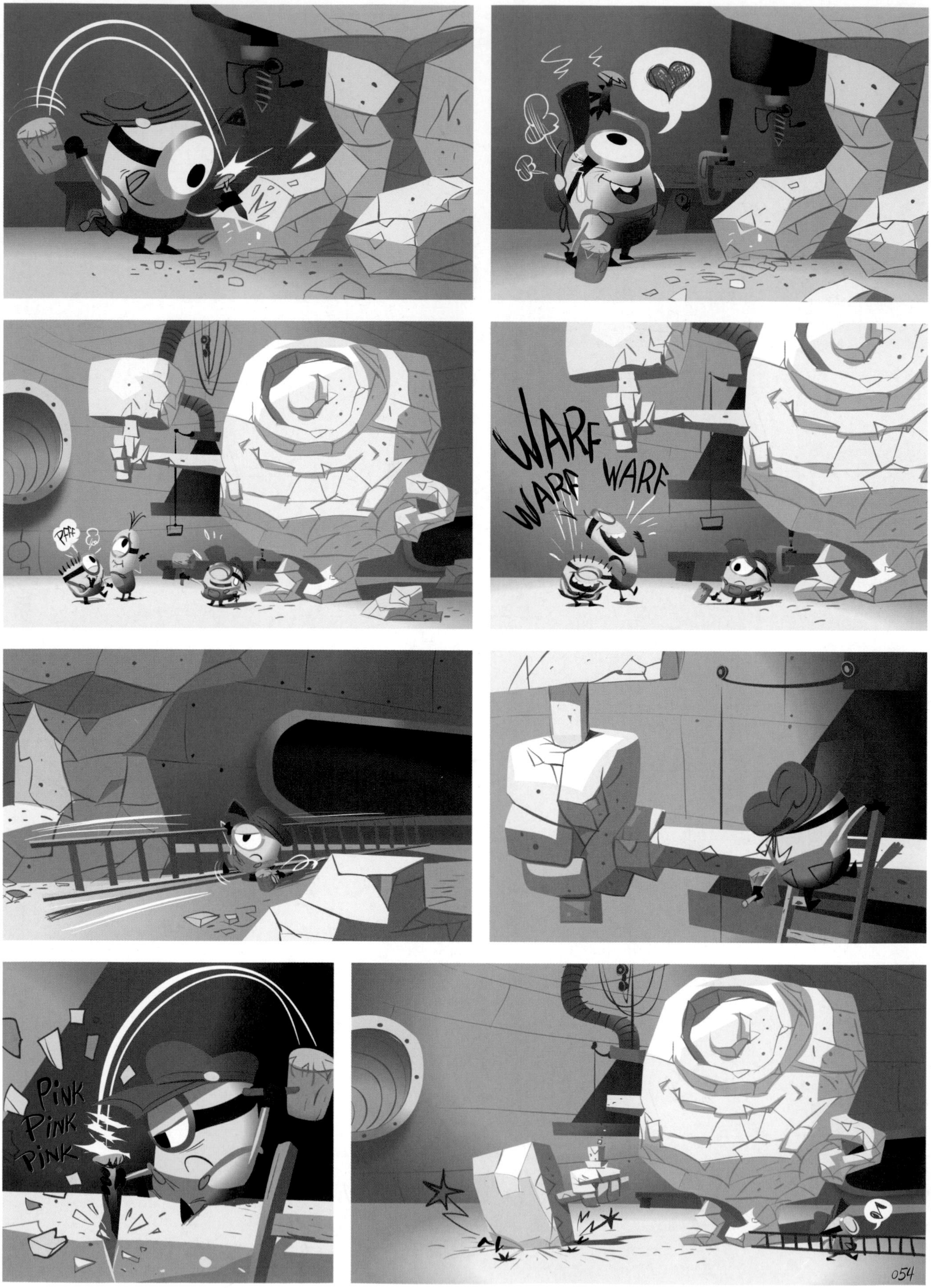
PFFF
WARF
WARF
WARF
WARF
PINK
PINK
PINK
054
RENAUD + LAPUSS' 2015

BANANA BAR

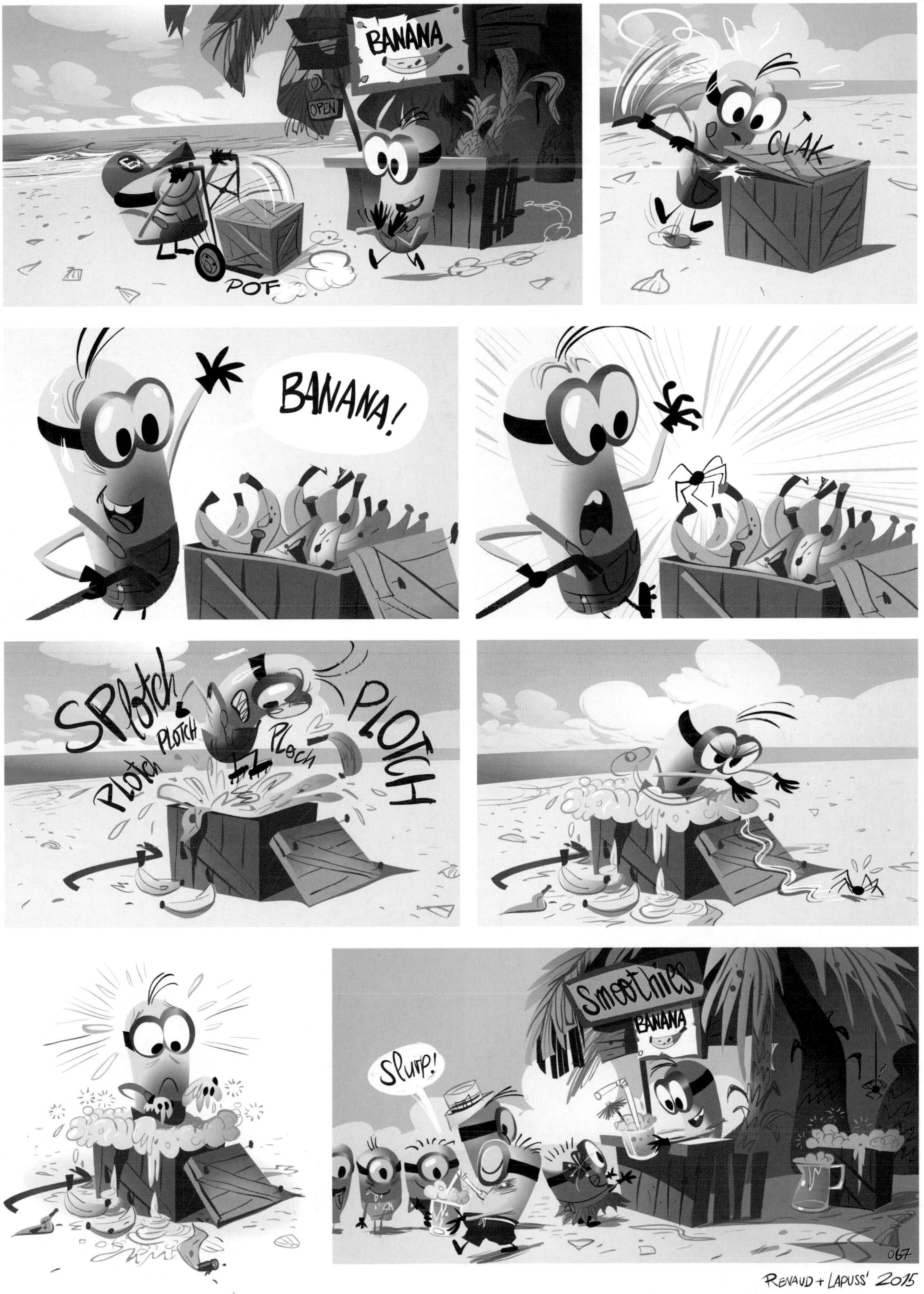
BANANA
OPEN
POF
CLAK
BANANA!
SPlotch
PLOTCH
Plotch
Ploch
PLOTCH
Smoothies
BANANA
Slurp!

RENAUD + LAPUSS' 2015

HEADPHONE ATTACK

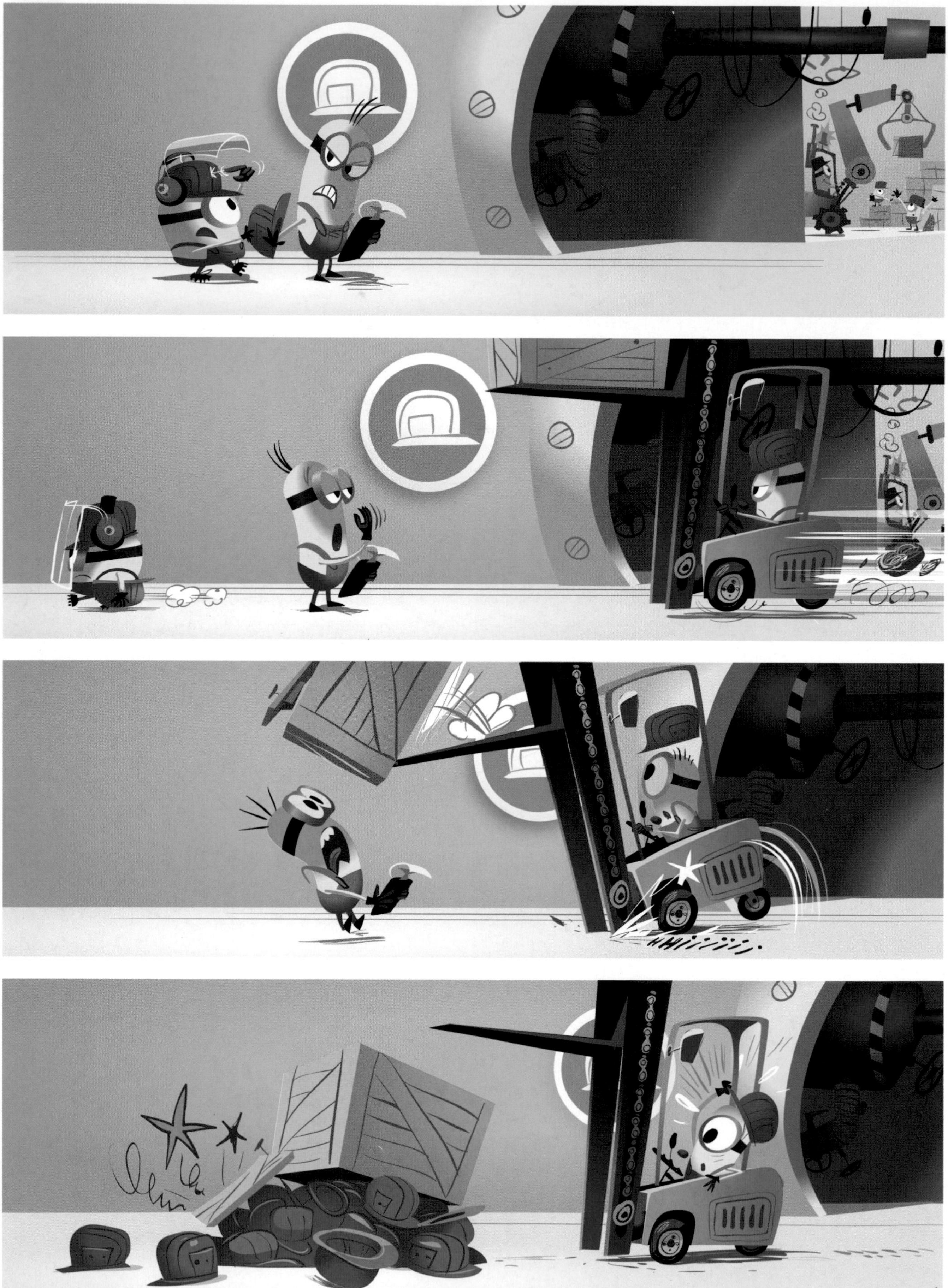

RENAUD + LAPUSS' 2015

EXPRESS STORAGE

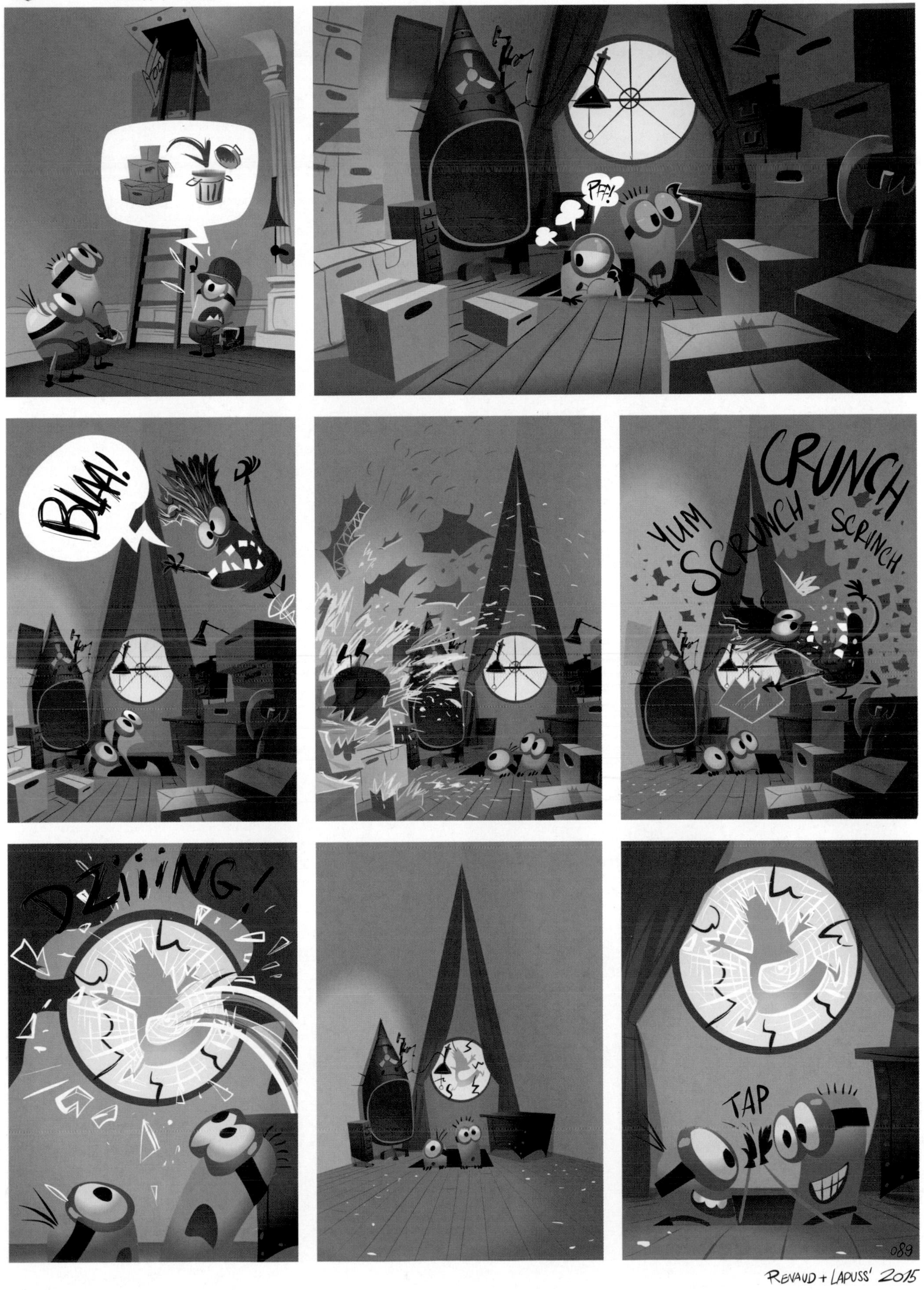
PFF!
BLAA!
CRUNCH
YUM
SCRUNCH
SCRINCH
DZIIING!
TAP

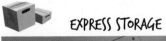

RENAUD + LAPUSS' 2015

DRY CLEANING

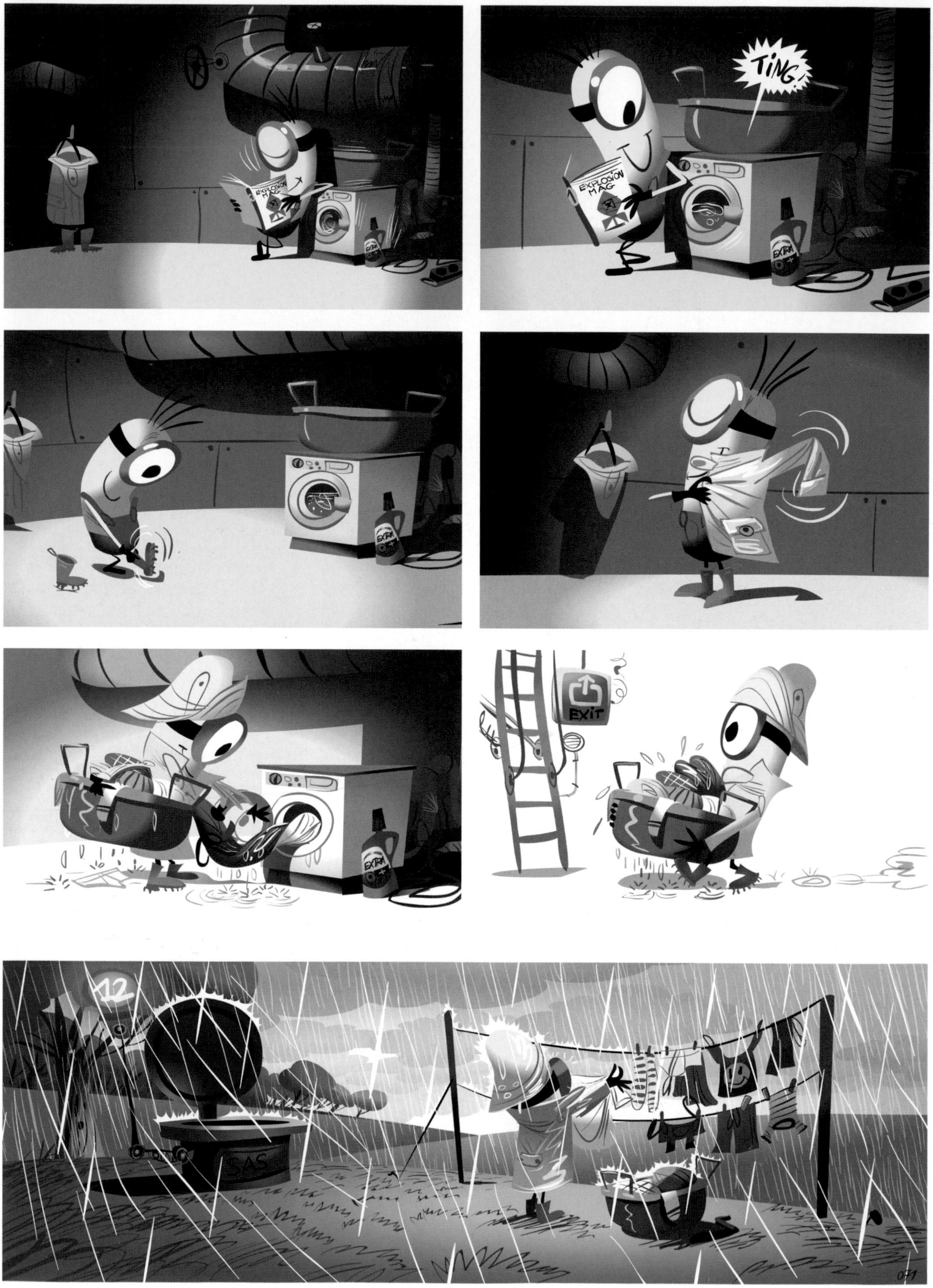
EXPLOSION MAG
EXPLOSION MAG
TING!
EXTRA
EXIT
12
SAS

RENAUD + LAPUSS' 2015

THE SAUCE

YUMYUM!
THE SAUCE!
Spotch
Spotch
Spotch
CRUNCH
CRUNCH
FIRE ALARM
CLAK
BEE DOO! BEE DOO!
Clic
Clic
Clic
BUNK!
CLAP!

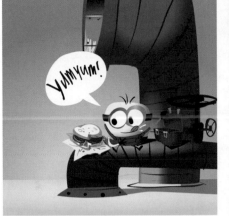

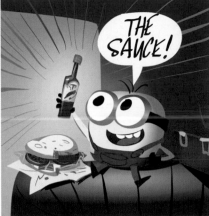

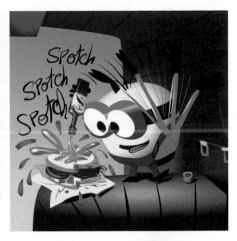

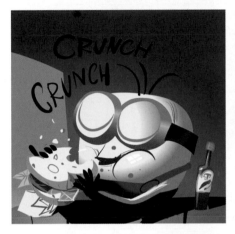

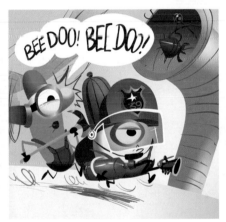

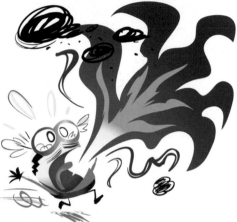

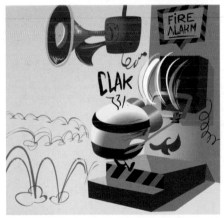

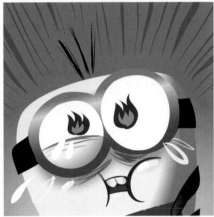

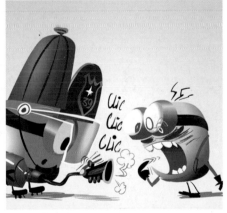

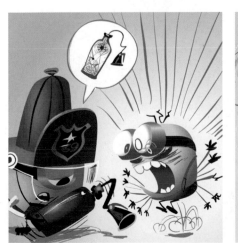

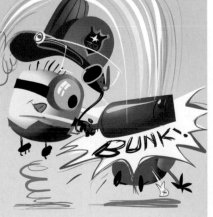

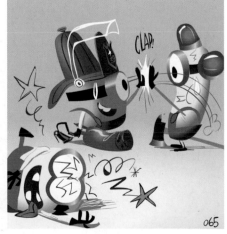

RENAUD + LAPUSS' 2015

WHAT'S HOT!

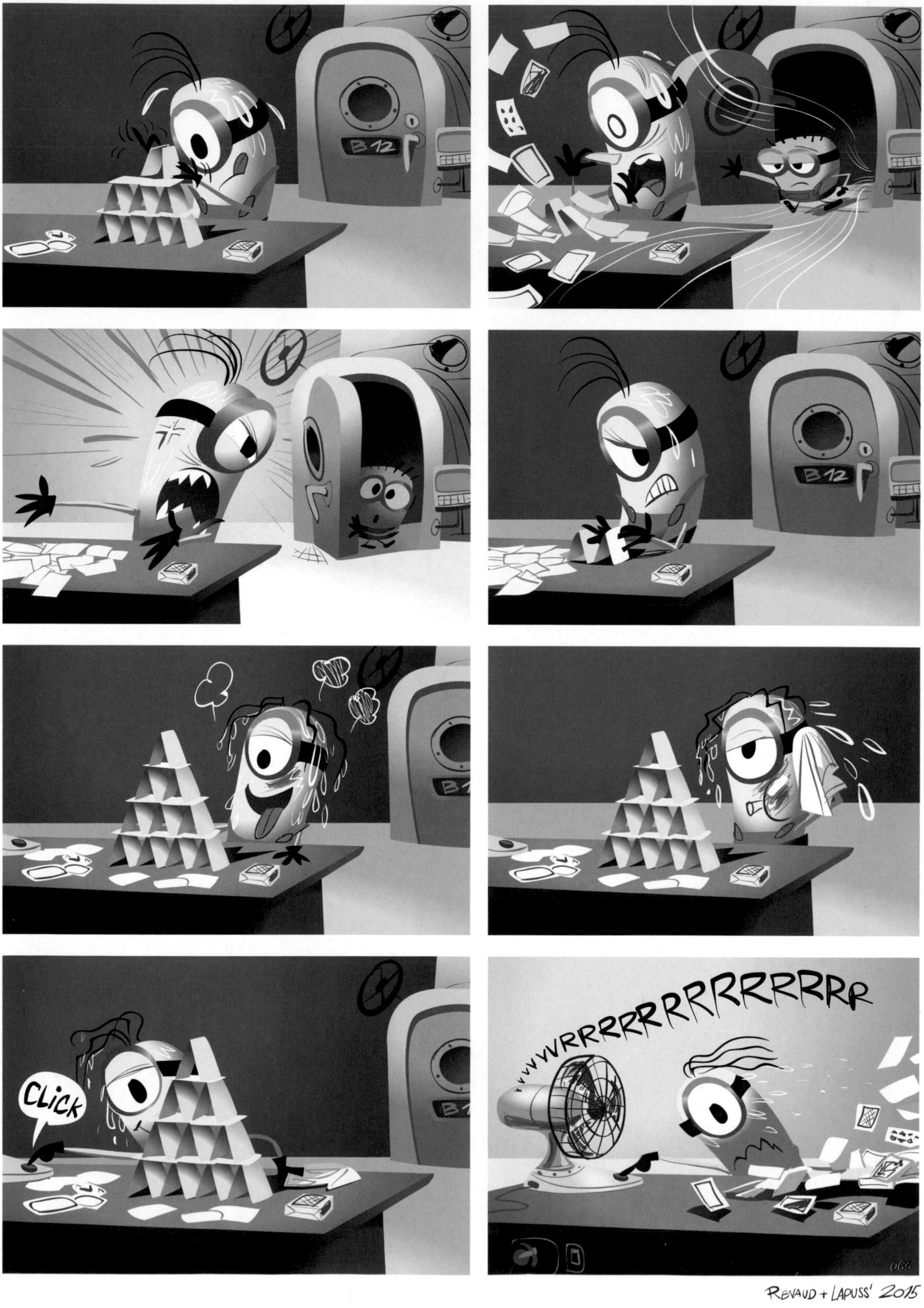

B12
B12
CLICK
vvvvvVRRRRRRRRRRRRRR

RENAUD + LAPUSS' 2015

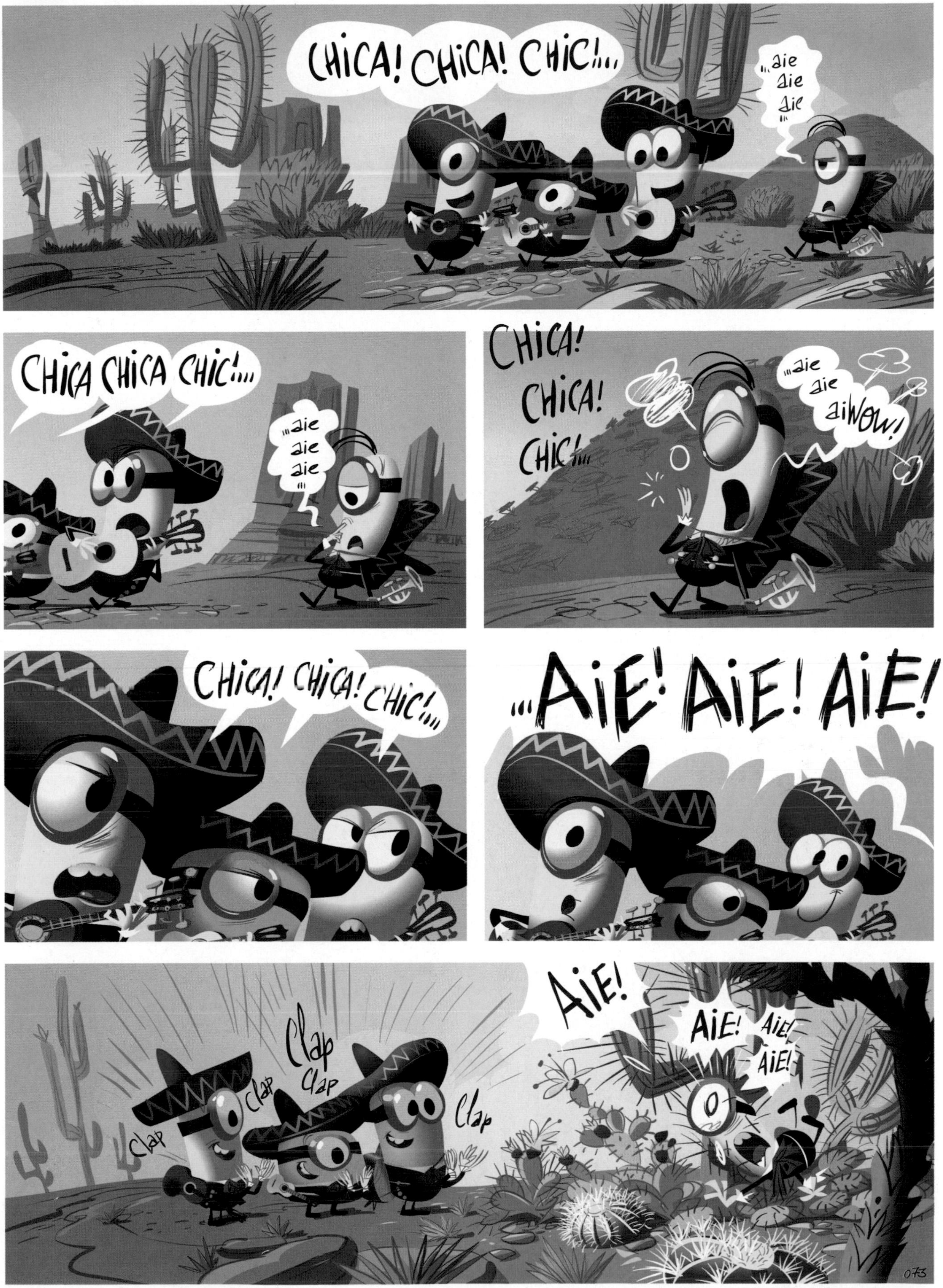
CHICA! CHICA! CHIC!...
...aie aie aie ...
CHICA CHICA CHIC!...
...aie aie aie ...
CHICA! CHICA! CHIC!...
...aie aie aiWOW!
CHICA! CHICA! CHIC!...
...AiE! AiE! AiE!
Clap
Clap
Clap
Clap
Clap
AiE!
AiE!
AiE!
AiE!
073

RENAUD + LAPUSS' 2015

DOUBLE PICKLES

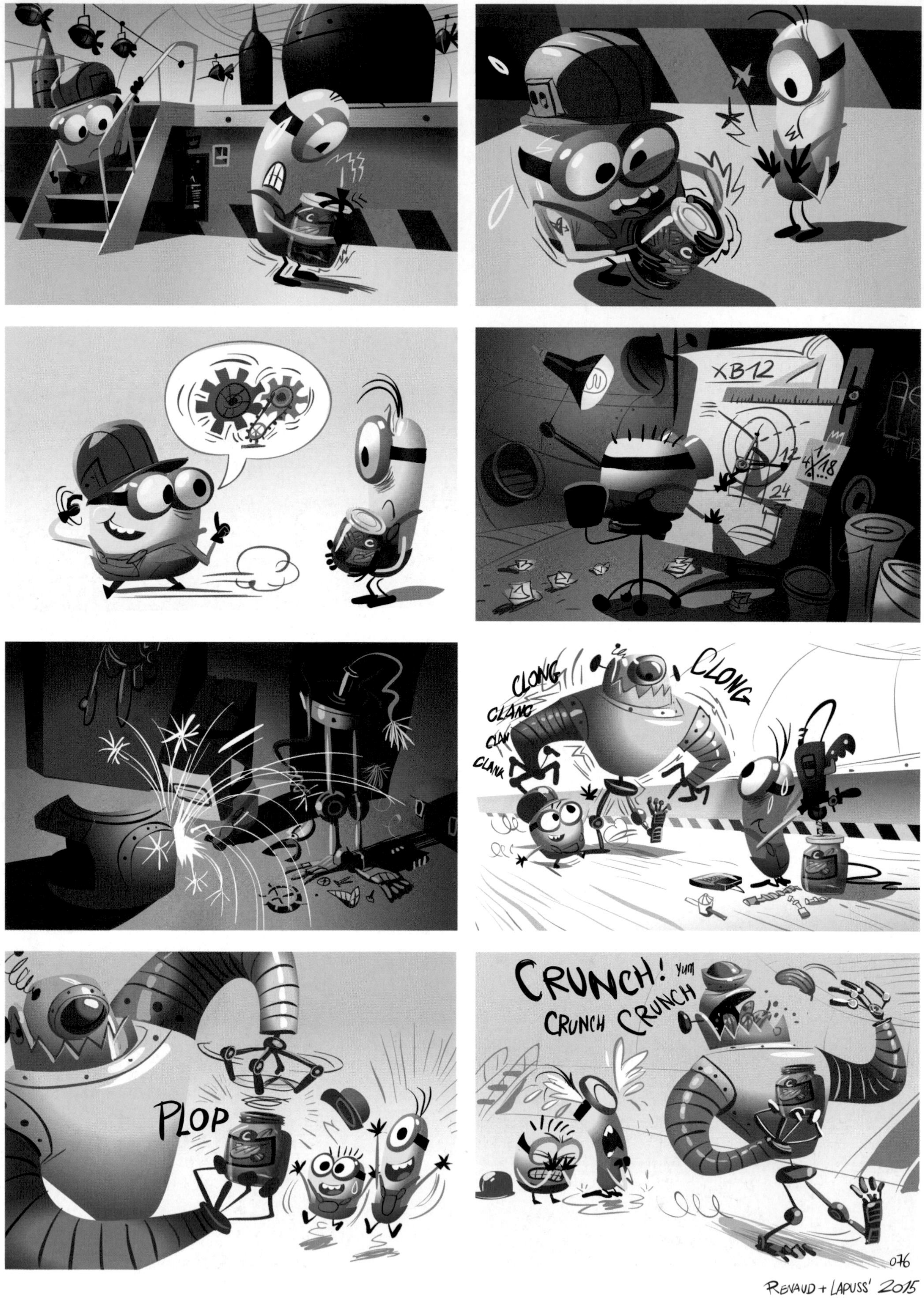
XB12
CLONG
CLANG
CLANK
CLONG
PLOP
CRUNCH! yum
CRUNCH CRUNCH

RENAUD + LAPUSS' 2015

GREEDY

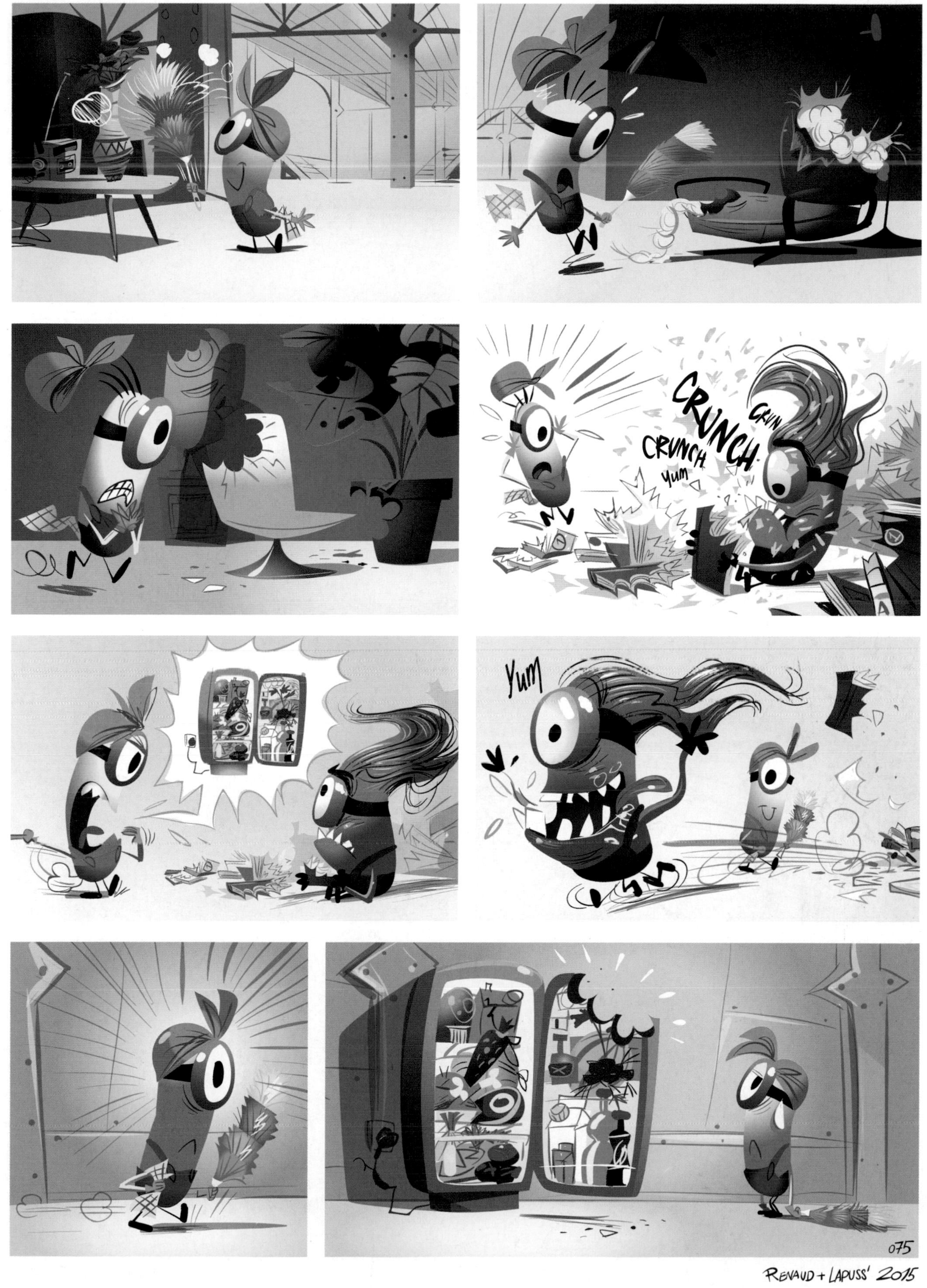
CRUNCH
CRUN
CRUNCH
yum
Yum

RENAUD + LAPUSS' 2015

CHINESE SHADOWS

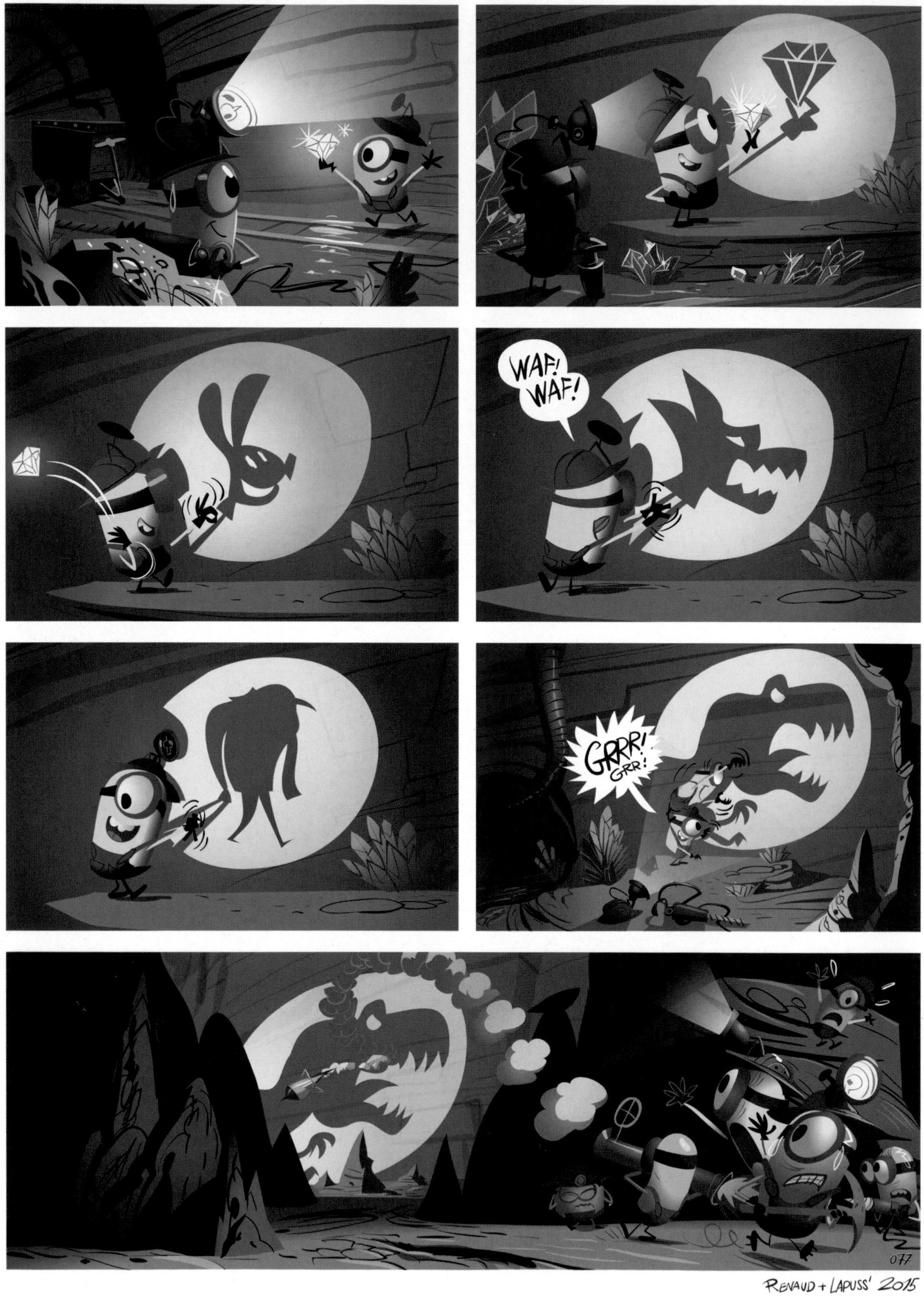
WAF! WAF!
GRRR! GRR!
077

RENAUD + LAPUSS' 2015

FLOWER POWER

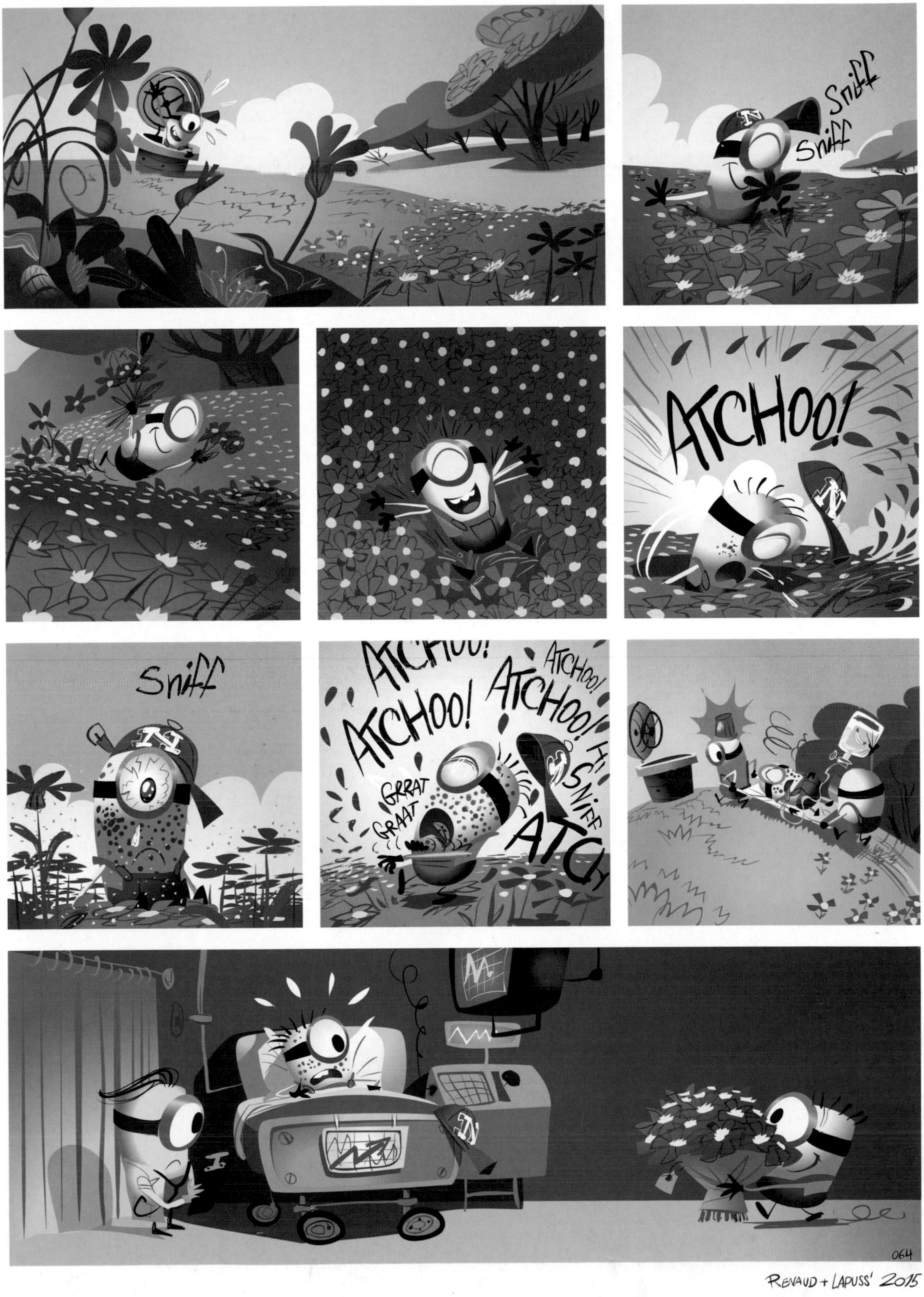
Sniff
Sniff
ATCHOO!
Sniff
ATCHOO!
ATCHOO!
ATCHOO!
GRRAT
GRAAT
SNIFF

RENAUD + LAPUSS' 2015

EVIL BASKET

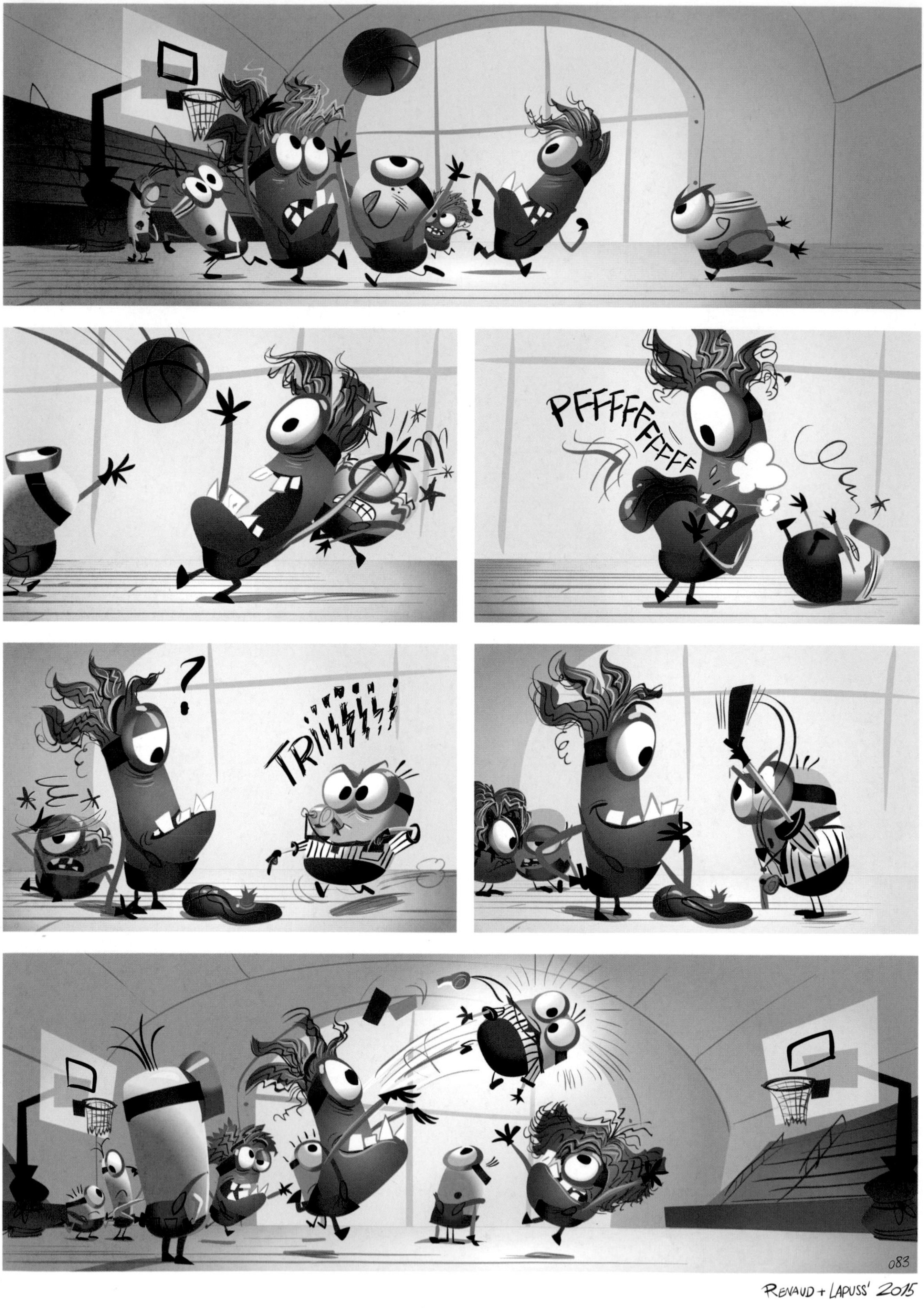
PFFFFFFFFFFF
?
TRiiii!!!!

RENAUD + LAPUSS' 2015

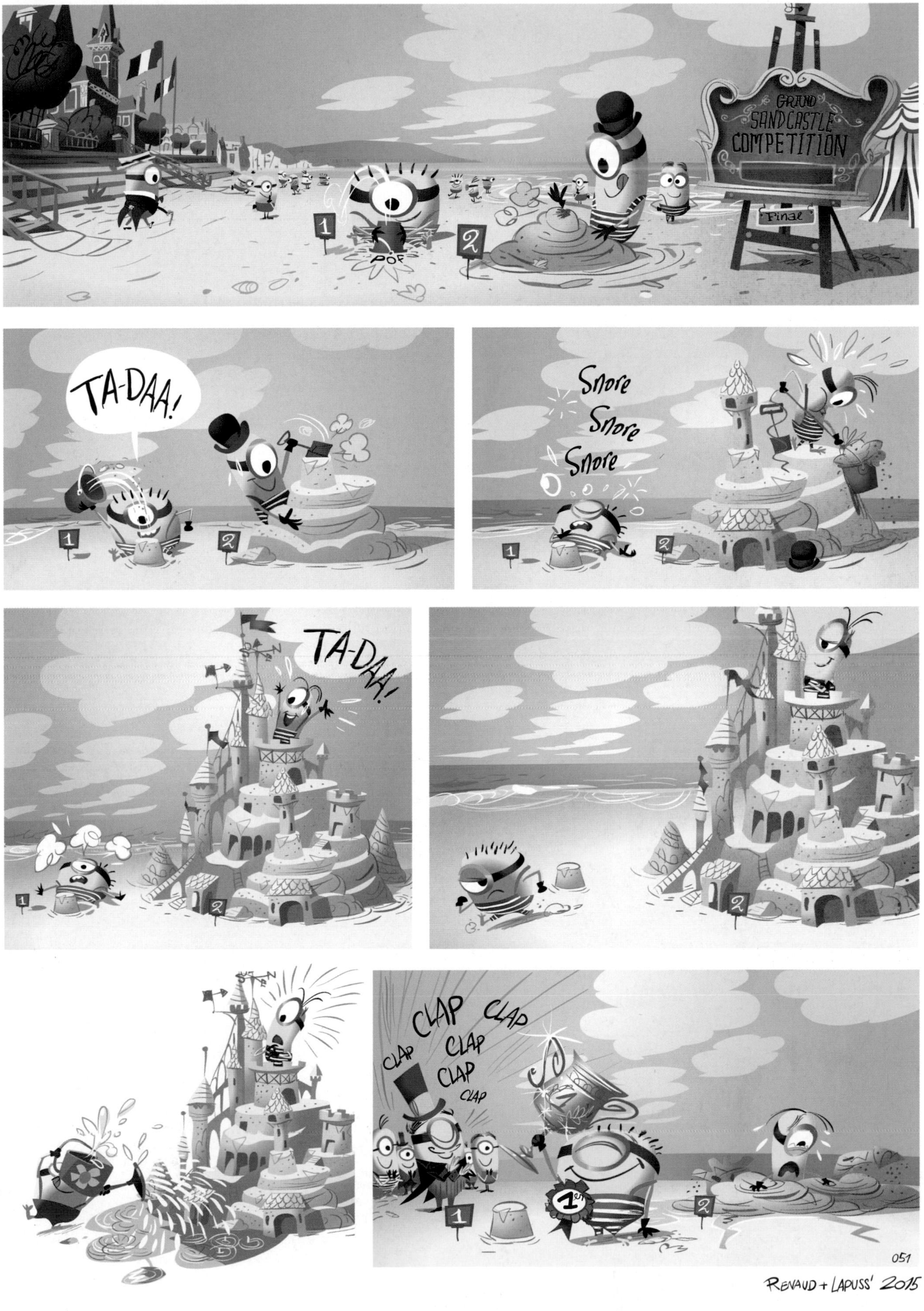
GRAND SANDCASTLE COMPETITION
Final
1
POP
2
TA-DAA!
1
2
Snore
Snore
Snore
1
2
TA-DAA!
1
2
1
2
CLAP
CLAP
CLAP
CLAP
CLAP
CLAP
1er
1
2

RENAUD + LAPUSS' 2015

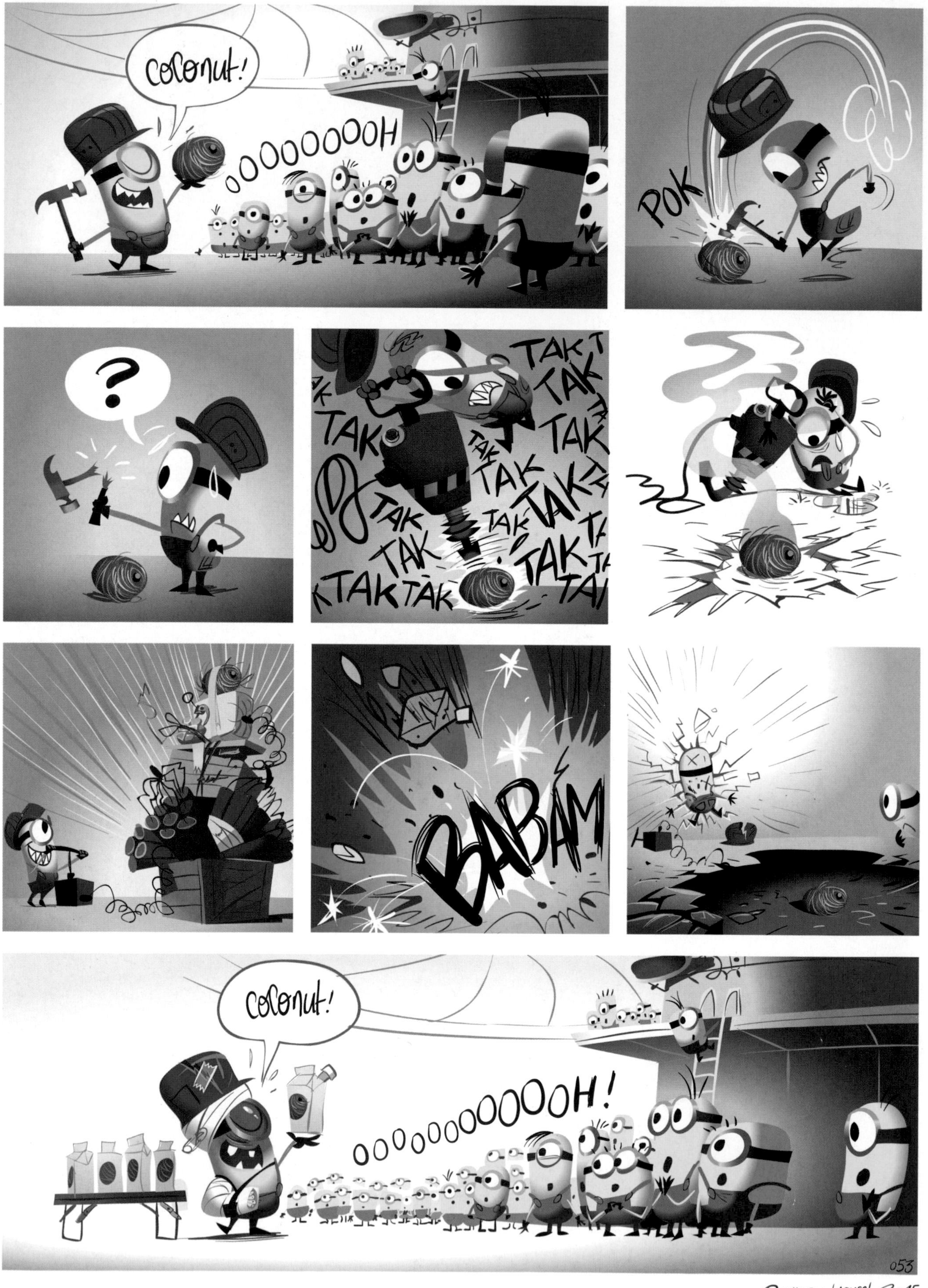
Coconut!
OOOOOOOOOH
POK
?
TAK TAK TAK TAK TAK TAK TAK TAK TAK TAK TAK TAK TAK
BABAM
Coconut!
OOOOOOOOOOOOOOH!

RENAUD + LAPUSS' 2015

ROCKABILLY BANANA

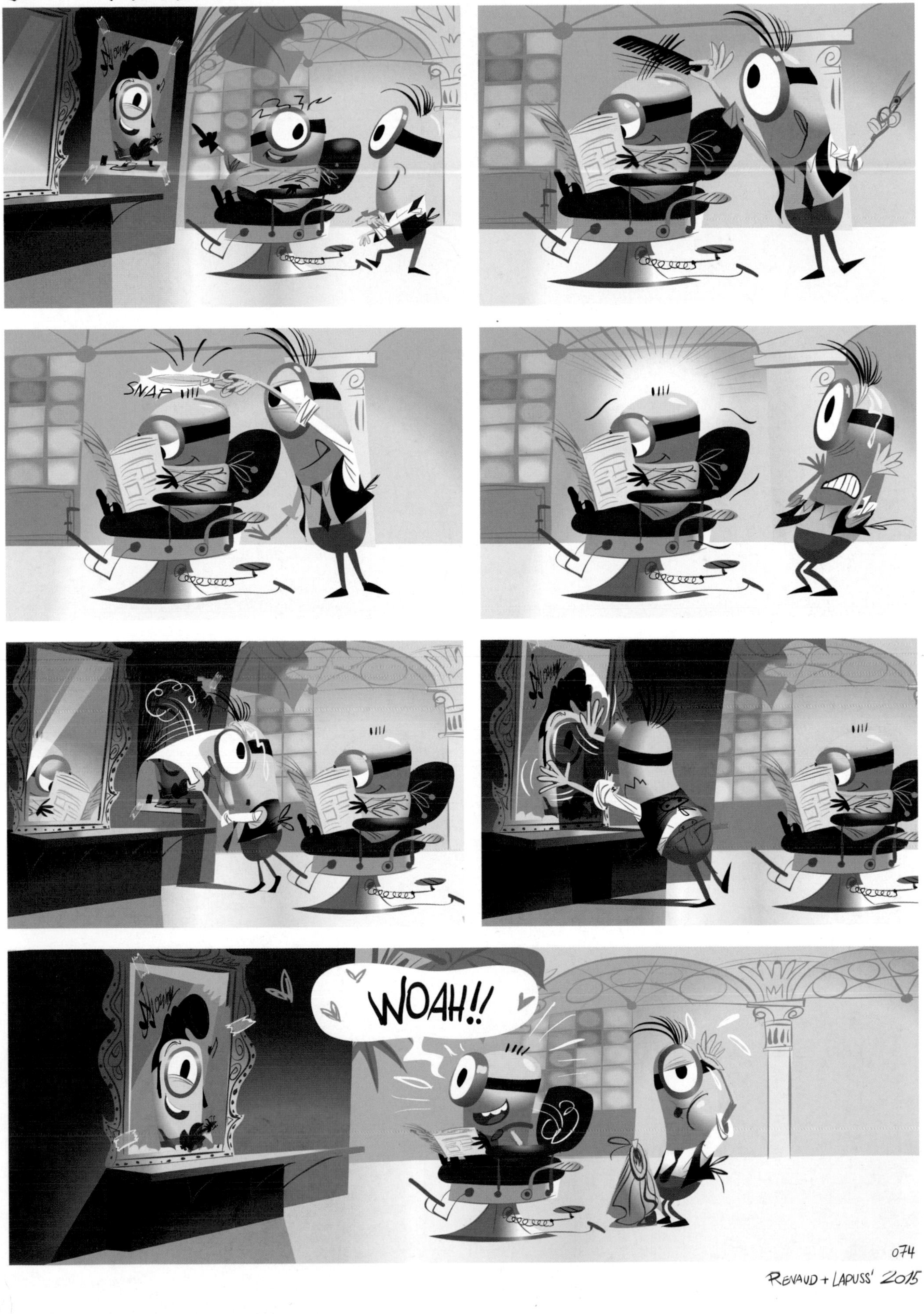

SNAP
WOAH!!

RENAUD + LAPUSS' 2015

TAKE AIM!

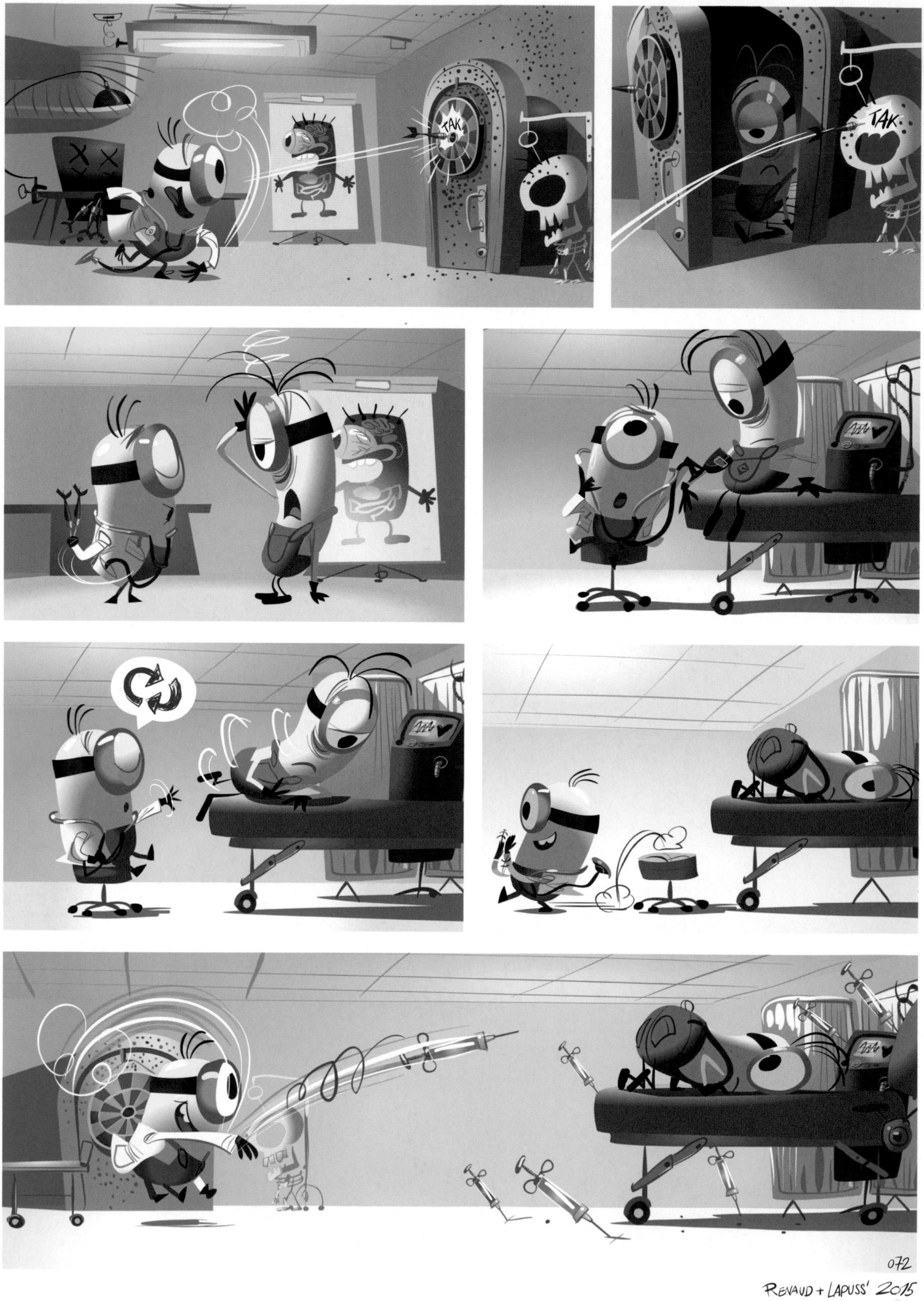
TAK
TAK

RENAUD + LAPUSS' 2015

THE PISTOL

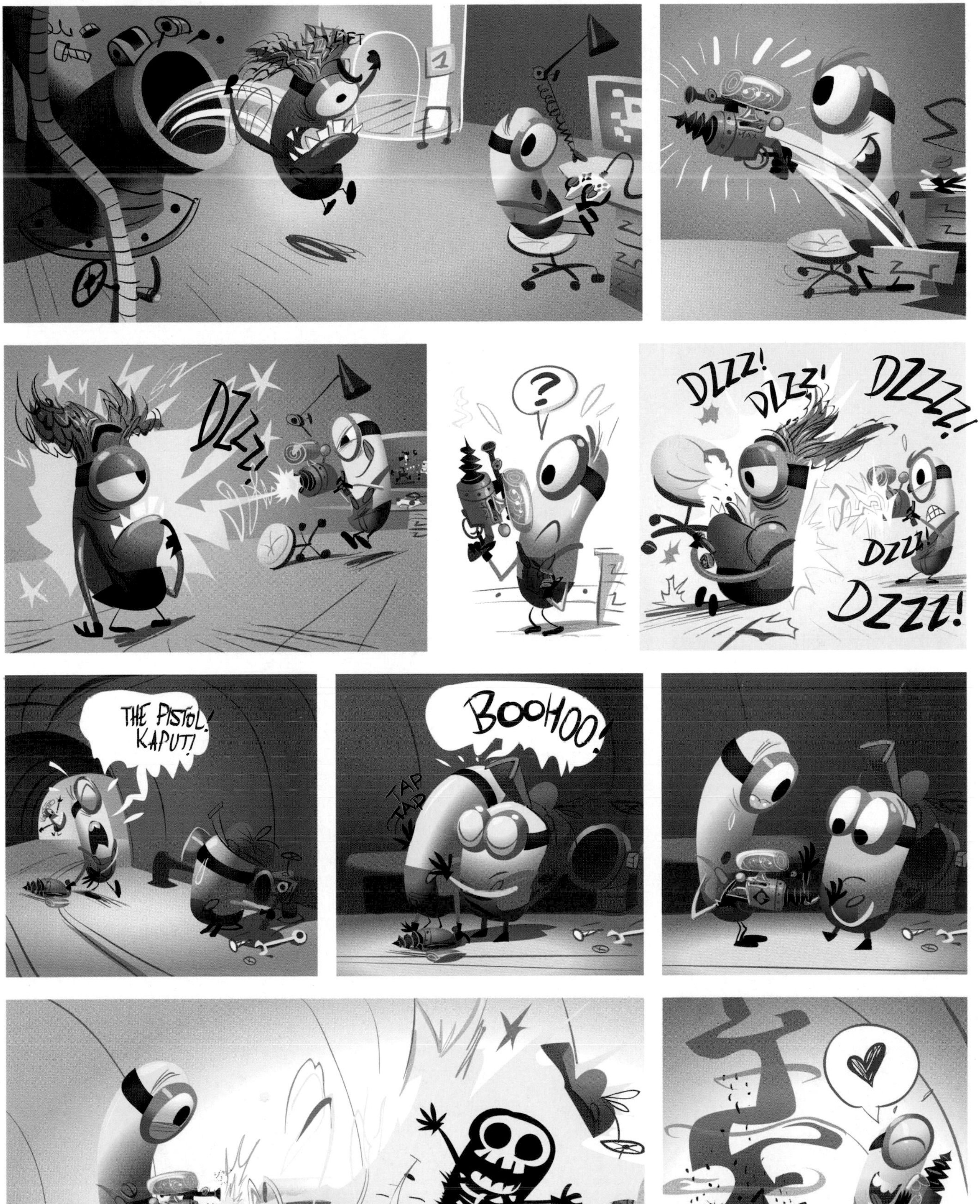
DZZZ!
?
DZZZ!
DZZZ!
DZZZZZ!
DZZZ!
DZZZ!
THE PISTOL! KAPUT!
TAP TAP
BOOHOO!

REVAUD + LAPUSS' 2015

FATAL ROT

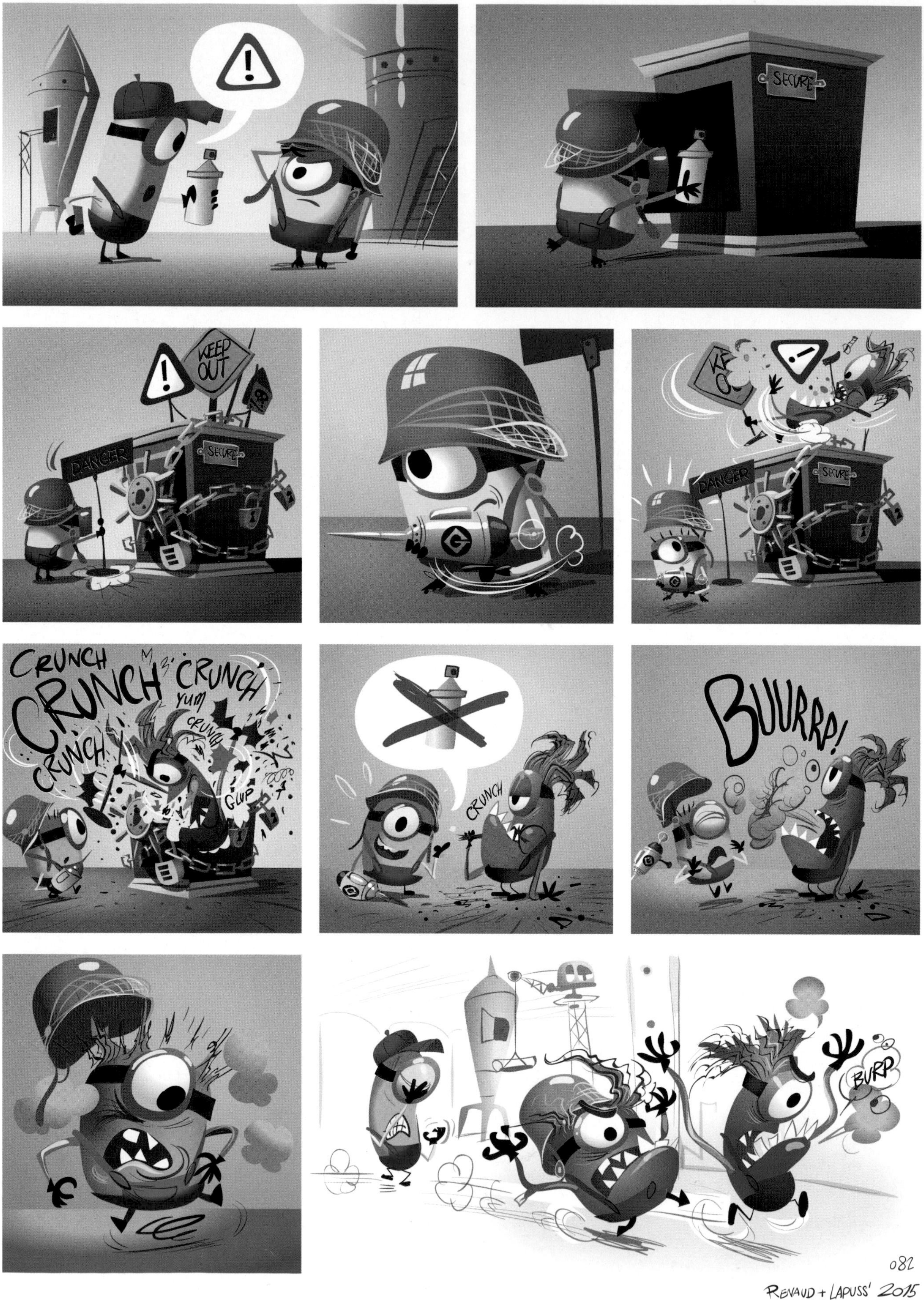
SECURE
KEEP OUT
DANGER
SECURE
DANGER
SECURE
CRUNCH
CRUNCH
CRUNCH
CRUNCH
yum
CRUNCH
GLUP
CRUNCH
BUURRP!
BURP

RENAUD + LAPUSS' 2015

ANTIDOTE

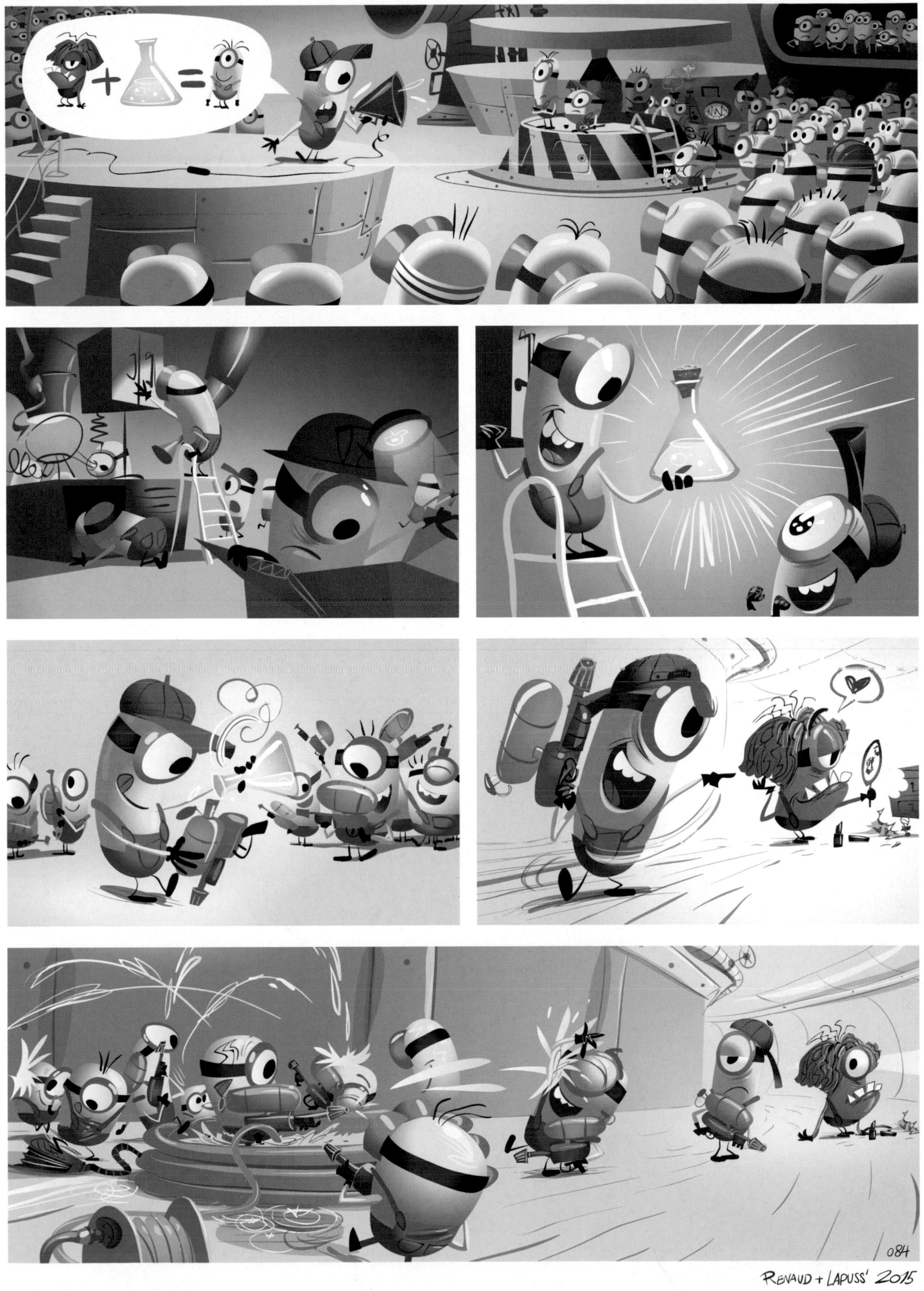

RENAUD + LAPUSS' 2015

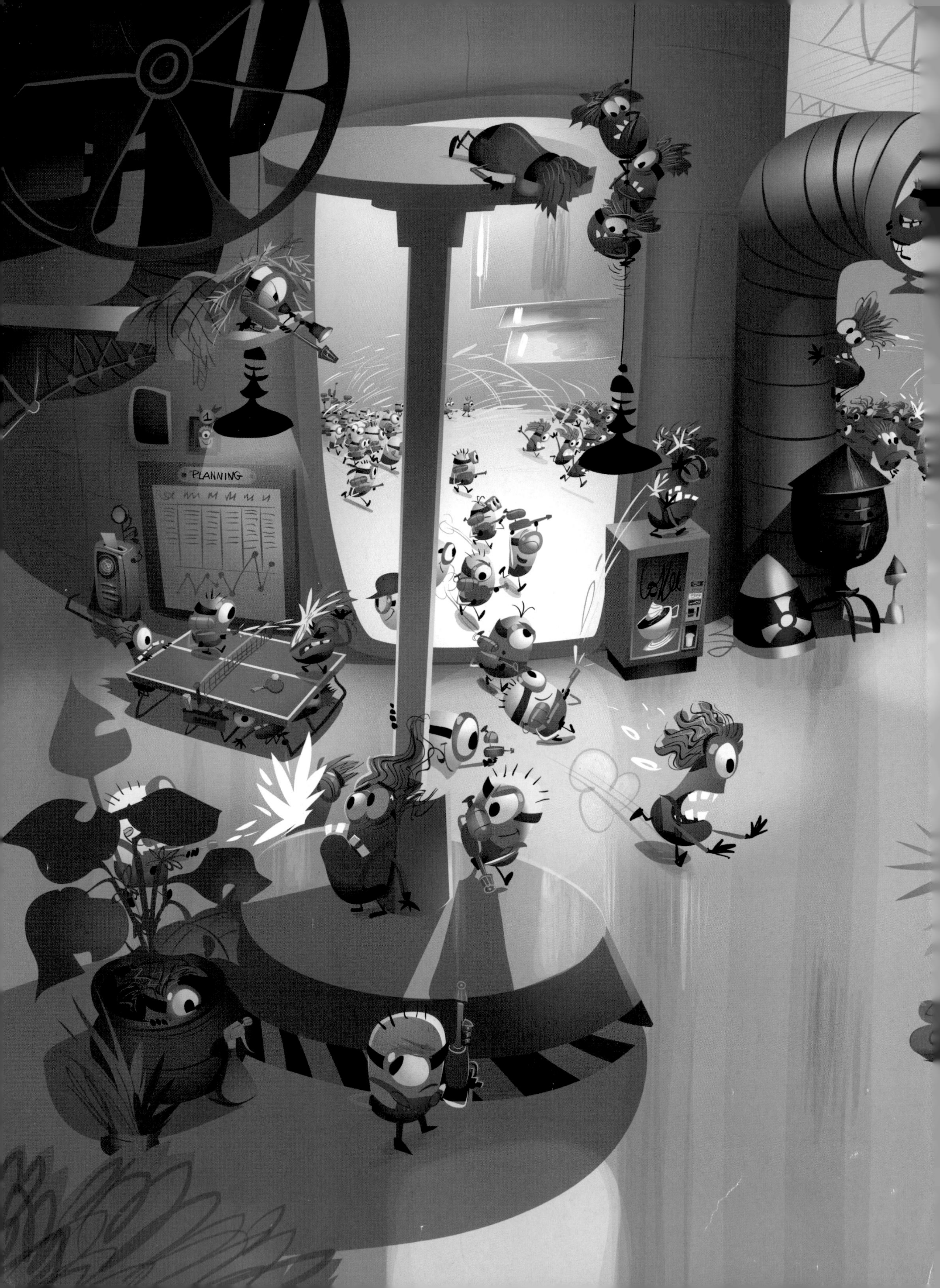
PLANNING

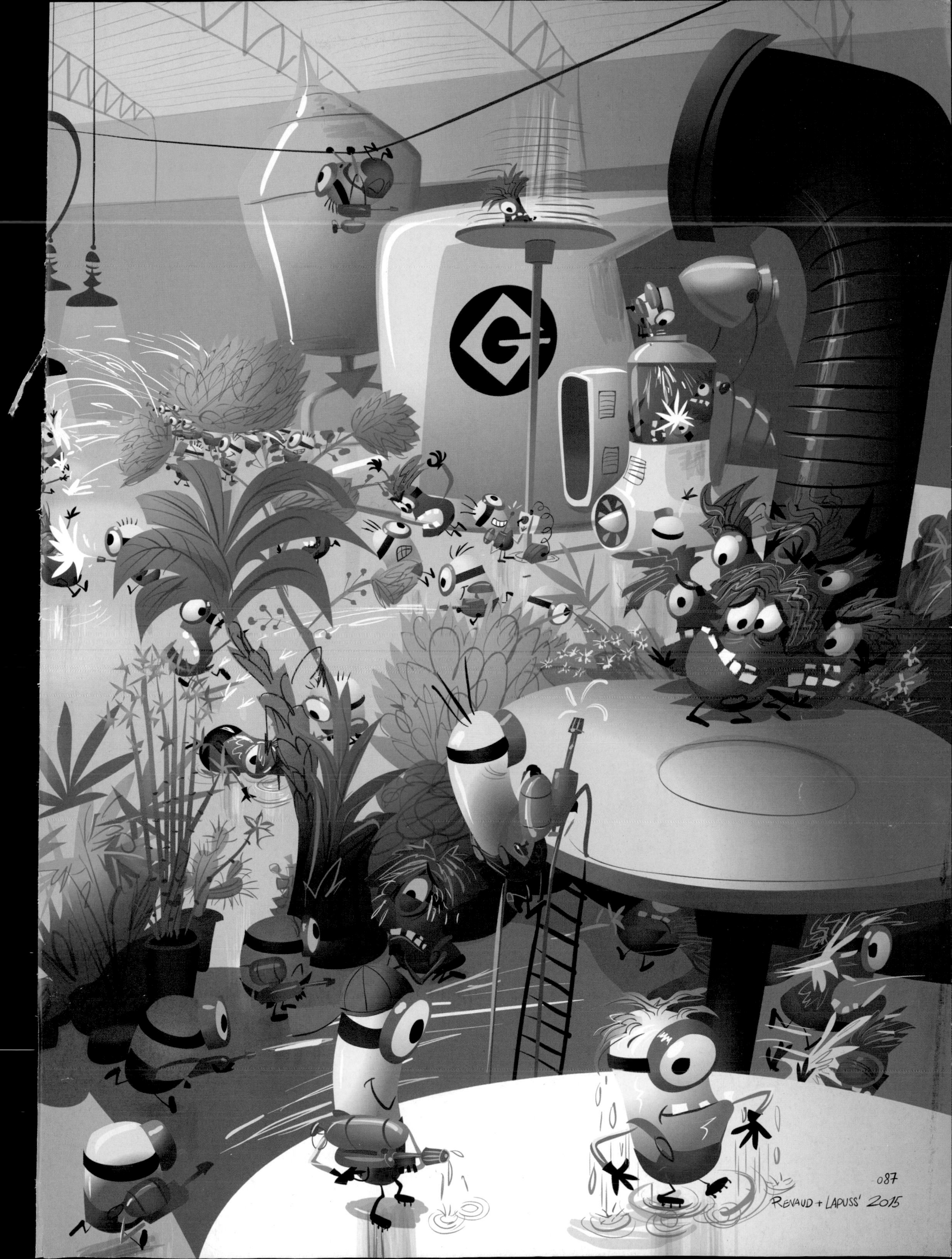
RENAUD + LAPUSS' 2015

PAINT JOKE

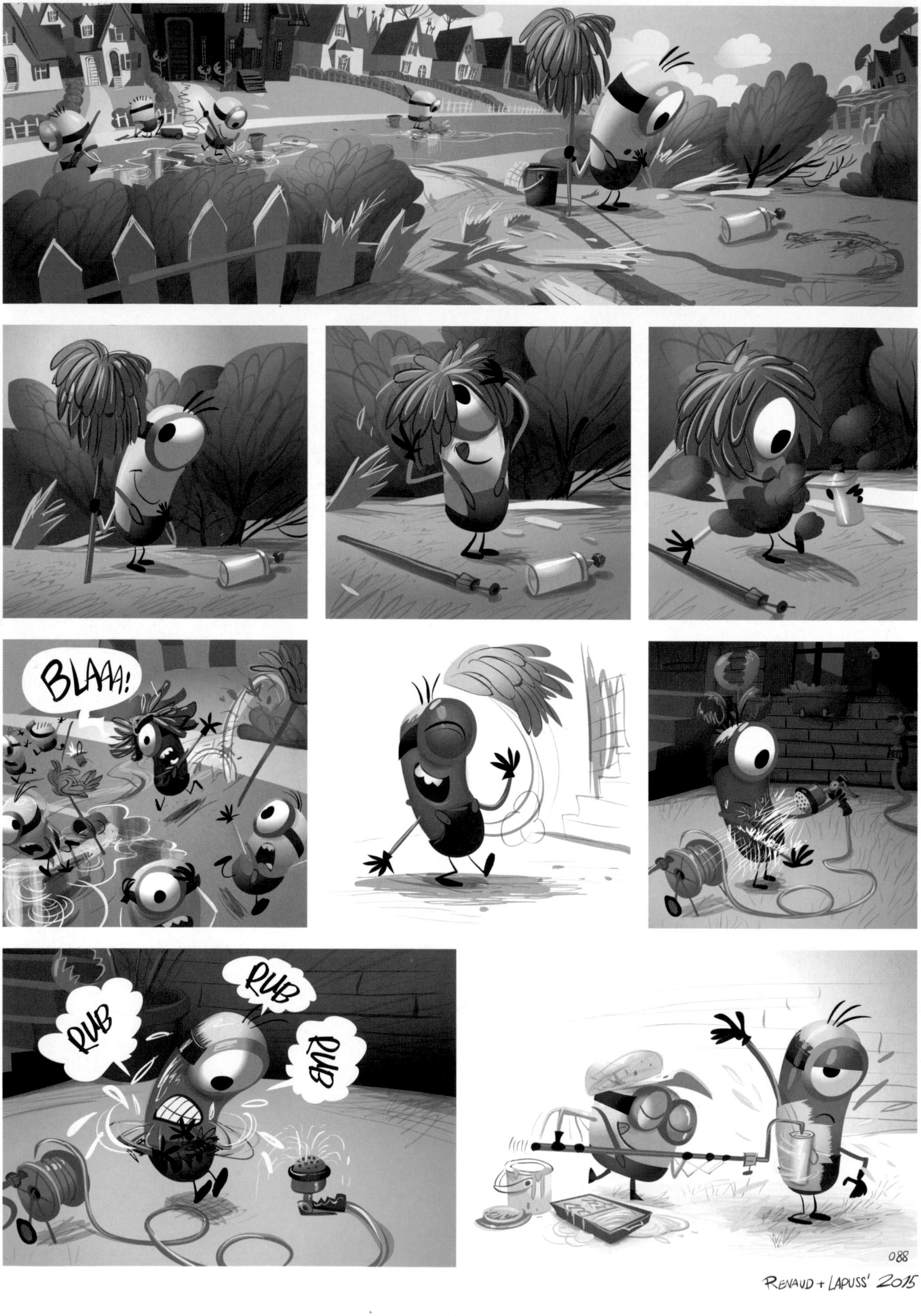
BLAAA!
RUB
RUB
RUB

RENAUD + LAPUSS' 2015